Thank you for the support! Enjoy it!

Reality

By

Shanaetris S. Jones

Shanaetris S. Jones

A Second Time Media & Communications Book/published by arrangement with the author(s).

Printing History

First printing: August 2010

Cover design and production by Miller Design Studio

For bulk order information address:

Second Time Media & Communications LLC,

P.O. Box 401367

Redford, MI 48240-1367

800-377-7479

ISBN: 978-0-9840660-9-4

SECOND TIME MEDIA COMMUNICATIONS

www.secondtimemedia.com

Dedication

I would love to dedicate this book to the ones who are no longer with me in the physical, but in spirit. Larry Smith, Teeya Riley, Christopher Newsome, Jimmel Maddox, Michael D. Johnson and My Late Great Grandfathers.

To the two who inspired this book Elroy Jones and Nathaniel Haynes.

To my loving family and friends thank you so much for your love and support. You guys saw my vision before I did.

To my heart and soul, Christina Collins: Words are not enough to express my love for you. Thank you and Michael for showing me unconditional love. I'm truly blessed to have parents like you both.

To my great-great grandmother Alice, you're God's gift to me. I love you. Thank you for all the wisdom and courage that has kept me going.

To all the Jones women and men, you have just help build another powerful intelligent woman. Thank you!

To my #1 fans, Shakeima Jackson, Willie Horton, Erica N. Jones and Latoya Smith. Thank you for pushing me.

My message to everyone is no dream is too big to accomplish. Never give up, no matter what! Make your dreams into a *Reality*!!!

Humbly,

Shanaetris S. Jones

Prologue

I couldn't help but wonder how I'd gotten myself into this situation. As I sat in the sterile, all white room, tremors of fear ran through my body. I couldn't be mad at anyone but myself. I had been through so much in my eighteen years; if I told the story anyone would think I was at least twenty-five.

I strolled down memory lane as I waited for the doctor to come in and administer my abortion. I had been hurt by the only man I had given my heart to. As far as family, my mother had been the only one who had stood in the gap when times were tough for me. My sperm-donor gave me reason to proudly sing the Tierra Marie song, 'No Daddy.' People could say I was a 'teen gone wild,' but really I was a young girl looking for love and surviving in the streets on instinct alone.

My leg started to shake as I watched the door knob turn. My time had come. The nurse signaled that my room was ready and that I should follow her. As I walked into the room I felt like I was walking straight into the devil's plan. I had let myself fall to the lowest point of my life, and I didn't want my unborn child to suffer for the mistakes I'd made. I needed to take control of my life and get back on track.

"Here you are," the nurse said handing me a gown to put on. "You can change in there."

Nervously I answered, "Um...I think I need more time. I'm not sure this is really what I want to do." I handed her back the gown and headed to the door.

When I walked back into the lobby, I looked at all the girls that sat there just as nervous as I had been just minutes ago. I hoped that the look on my face might change the mind of the ones that were undecided.

I walked out to the parking lot and noticed there was a white note taped to my car window. I opened the note and it read, "*Remember one who does wrong, must not go unpunished.*" I looked around wondering who had placed it on my window. Though the lot was full, no one was sitting in the cars. I brushed it off and jumped into my car.

My cousin Kyle always said, "What goes around comes around." I knew eventually the things I'd done were going to catch up to me, but I wasn't prepared for the storm that lurked ahead of me.

I pulled all the way to the back and used the back door. I had built my courage up and was going to tell my mother everything that I had done. Then I was going to get myself together. She wasn't home yet, so I lied back on my bed and reminisced about the past few years. Let's just say I never saw myself ending up here. Let me take you back to the beginning.

Chapter One

Who am I you ask? I'm Ar'monnie Nay'onna Wright. Born to a loving and caring family which I felt I had been absolutely blessed with. I came into the world with a silver spoon in my mouth. I never had to work for anything. I got good grades so I got good gear. My mama and cousins had me living the good life. I feared nothing but not getting what I wanted.

I got so much love from my girls, Jade, Kristin and Kiyah. Kiyah was my right hand. She made sure I saw my way through every challenge I faced. I lived in a world that had no problems and no worries. Most people believe if a girl doesn't have a father present growing up she has a void in her that can never be filled. Well my father wasn't around but my cousins filled that spot. It wasn't a big deal that my father wasn't there. I was going to make it with or without him.

The summer of 99' was when, as the older folks would say, 'I started smelling myself.'

"This summer is ours Monnie !We about to be seniors," my girl Kiyah sang as we stood in front of my house. Kiyah was a thick chick, but she reminded everyone of Penny from "Good Times."

"I know! I'm so excited! Ricardo or Kyle better get me a car 'cause I know if my mom gets it, it's not going to be anything I want to drive," I said shaking my head at the thought of what kind of car she would pick. I pulled my hair back into a ponytail. I was petite with a honey brown complexion. My girl's said I looked like Kyla Pratt.

My older cousin's Ricardo and Kyle were my mother's brother's sons. Ricardo was 19, and Kyle was 21. They were the predominant male figures in my life. They both looked out for me and my mom made sure I had everything a girl could want and need. Even though they were 'in the streets,' they made sure that their family was tight. I felt safe when they were around. Ricardo was the cool one and Kyle was more the father type but they both could work a nerve, if you ask me.

"Yo, you stupid!" Jade said laughing at my remark. Jade was the dark skinned girl in our group. Most of the guys our age would always tell her, she was so pretty to be dark; which she hated to hear. But, she was full of herself and was always lying. That girl would lie in front of Jesus if she had to! "So, Ms. Cass Tech what you got planned?" Jade asked Kristin pushing her on the arm playfully.

Kristin was a short redbone with freckles. Her "D" cup breast had all the middle school boys following behind her but Kristin was a good girl. I was so proud of her though, she kept her head in them books unlike the rest of us. We did just enough to get by, but Kristin went to the extreme and wanted more for herself.

"I have homework to do from my orientation," she looked down at her finger nails. Me. Kiyah and Jade looked at each other like she was crazy.

"Damn Kristin, you so lame!" Kiyah yelled out and we all burst out laughing.

This was the life. Living, laughing and being around nothing but love. I never knew how much it meant until I wasn't getting it anymore.

Reality

After an hour or so the girls left, and I was home alone. I thought about calling my boyfriend Rico to come over, but he never seemed to answer his phone when he was in the streets. Rico and I had just started dating seriously though we had been friends since 3rd grade.

Rico just did it for me! Even though he wasn't the best boyfriend there was something about him that I loved so much. I guess it may have been the fact that I made him wait so long to even give him a chance. He had been hounding me to be in a relationship since ninth grade but it wasn't until the end of this year that I gave in.

Rico was what they called a 'Corner boy.' He sold drugs on the corners and out of crack houses. His goal was to make his way up the totem pole by any means necessary. The money he made now kept him in fresh gear and able to throw a little money around but he had higher aspirations. My friends couldn't stand him but that didn't matter to me. All that mattered was how much I loved him and how much he loved me. Only I knew how he really felt for me.

I dialed his number and it rang once and went to the voicemail. 'He must be busy,' I thought to myself and lied back on my bed to watch some television. I left my phone right next to me so I could hear it ring if I fell asleep. That call never came that night.

Chapter Two

The next morning I woke up to my mom listening to Anita Baker's "*Body N Soul.*" Walking to the bathroom, I could hear her and someone else down stairs talking.

"Mama? Who are you talking to?" I asked peeking over the banister.

"It's me Nay'onna," Kyle hollered up the steps. He always called me by my middle name.

"Oh, I'll be down in a minute!" I knew whenever he came over he had something for me. I threw on my robe and rushed down stairs and was disappointed to find he had nothing.

"Sit down," Kyle pulled a chair out for me next to him. I started getting the feeling that whatever he and Lynda had up their sleeves was nothing good. "Ricardo supposed to be on his way," he said looking at his watch.

Across town, Ricardo was doing ninety up all the side streets. "Dog slow down!" Mack said holding on to the passenger door.

"I need to hurry up and take care of this business real quick. My aunt and Kyle are having a meeting with Ar'Monnie and I need to be there. She is growing up so damn fast. Did you talk to this nigga?" he asked Mack as he punched down on the pedal turning onto Woodward where he was supposed to meet this guy. He was already leery because he hadn't done much business with them and he didn't know them well. Mack had supposedly checked them out though.

"Well, don't kill us trying to get there!" Mack was scared for his life. He always was with Ricardo when it came to taking care of business. Mack was Ricardo's right hand man.

"Man trust me, I ain't trying to kill myself so just sit back and chill. I don't see these nigga's. Call 'em," Ricardo demanded as he pulled to the back of White Castle's and continued looking around.

"They ain't answering," Mack said closing his cell phone.

An eerie feeling came over Ricardo as he said, "Something ain't right." No sooner had he spoken those words three guys rushed the car with their guns drawn.

"Aye! Get out of the car nigga!" one of the guys shouted pointing a gun directly at Ricardo's head.

"Alright man, just chill out!" Ricardo said stepping out, while mentally trying to weigh his options. Another guy had Mack out of the car with his hands in the air while a third guy was pulling a bag of money from the back seat.

"That's all that's in there, I swear" Ricardo said as he saw the guy take the money from the back. He wasn't even concerned about the money, he just wanted to make sure he made it out of this situation safely so he could get back to his family.

"Shut up!" the guy growled touching his head with the tip of the gun. Mack and Ricardo gave each other a look, which signaled their next move. Ricardo and Mack both turned and punched the guys who had them at gun point. Both guys stumbled, losing their balance. The guns slipped out of their hands and they scrambled to get them.

Mack and Ricardo had already taken off running as fast as they could up back alleys ducking and dodging. Unfortunately the guys were back on their feet and had started shooting at them.

"Come on man," Ricardo said helping Mack over the fence. He spotted the guys getting closer and felt the bullets whizzing by. Just as Mack scaled the fence, Ricardo felt a stinging pain in his shoulder.

"Ahh...shit!" he yelled grabbing his shoulder just as another bullet hit him, this time in his leg. He fell to the ground.

"Come on, we can't stop!" Mack said pulling him up. Miraculously they made it around the corner in front of the Secretary of State.

Ricardo could hardly focus as he shouted instructions to Mack. "Dawg, call my aunty. Tell her I'm coming. I have to be there she said it's about Monnie man." Ricardo was leaning on the door, as the security guard came out to help.

"Man, we have to get you to the hospital first. Don't worry about Monnie, she is going to be alright," Mack said still looking around to make sure the guy's weren't still chasing them.

"Naw, fuck the hospital! Get me to my cousin, man. She thinks I'm coming and I can't let her down." Ricardo was talking lower with every word. Mack made him lie down on the sidewalk and ignored what he was saying.

Ricardo sat there with crazy thoughts going through his head. "Damn man. What if this is it for me? Who gon' take care of Monnie? Man, please give me strength."

Ten minutes later the ambulance was there and he was rushed to the nearest hospital.

Back at home, Monnie was listening to what she thought was the best news ever.

"You know Mrs. Mays, the lady that I've been taking care of? Well, her son would like to take her up north for two weeks. He's going to pay me extra to go up there with them. I'm not going to make you go stay with anybody because I trust you. This is your house and you should be at home," Lynda said looking at me. I was trying my best to hold my excitement in.

"I will be around and you know to call me or Ricardo if you need anything," Kyle assured me. I think they thought I was sad about her going away to work, but I was jumping up and down in the inside. "Free!" is what I was screaming.

"Okay," I stood up hoping this conversation was over, but I should have known better. If it's one thing my mother likes to do is talk.

"I want to discuss something else with you," she said as I sat right back down with a sigh. "I know you are a mature young lady but just know that what you do from here on out is going to reflect in your future. So think twice before you make a decision and plan ahead. Don't disappoint me, Ar'monnie," she looked me in my eyes and I didn't have to read between the lines. I knew exactly what she was saying.

While we waited for Ricardo, I went back up to my room and called the girls and let them in on my good news. I also let Kiyah in on one of my plans.

Reality

"So that girl thinking about losing that V-card, huh?" Kiyah said laughing in the phone.

"No, I mean…I don't know. I've been thinking about it," I said shyly. I heard my mom screaming and crying and rushed off the phone. "Kiyah, I gotta go!"

I ran down the stairs, "Ma, what's wrong?" I grabbed her arm for her to sit down. Kyle was on the phone yelling at whomever it was he was talking to. He had tears streaming down his face which really had me shook.

"Ricardo's been shot," my mom cried holding her face in her hands.

My body went numb. Suddenly everything went quiet around me as if I had gone deaf. I could no longer hear my mother crying or the television blaring. I stood there in the middle of the chaos and tried to comprehend what I had just heard. I had just talked to him, and he was on his way here to talk to me. The hot tears started rolling down my face but I knew I had to remain calm for both Kyle and my mom.

"Go get your things, he's at Henry Ford," Kyle said walking out the door. I ran to my room slipped some shoes on and joined them in the car.

When we pulled up to Henry Ford hospital a sense of dread permeated in the car. Henry Ford had the reputation of "You might check in alive, but you damn sure won't check out that way."

The emergency room was filled to capacity with other families that were either praying for good results or mourning the bad results. Half of those people were friends of Ricardo and Kyle's.

"Excuse me, I'm his aunt," Lynda said pushing her way to the information desk where the security guard sat. He looked much too old to be handling all the chaos around him. People were screaming at him trying to get information about Ricardo. The crowd got quiet when they noticed Kyle was walking behind my mom. I think they were trying to gauge his reaction to see what their next move should be.

The security guard looked up his room number and gave Lynda three visitor badges. We were silent as we rode up to the third floor. They were just rolling him into the room when the doors to the elevator opened. We all ran down to the room.

He was sitting up with bandages wrapped around his arm and one on his leg. He looked a little out of it but his face brightened up when he saw us walk into the room.

"Are you okay?" Lynda asked wiping the tears from her eyes and kissing him on the cheek. I stood back by the door. I was so nervous I didn't want to touch anything or mess anything up.

"Yea, Aunty I'm good." He smiled looking at her. "Come here lil' girl," he said glancing over at me.

I walked in slow and scared. "Give me a hug," he said leaning up in the bed. He grimaced a little so I was careful when I hugged him even though I wanted to give him the biggest bear hug I could muster up.

"I was so scared," I whispered in his ear trying to hold the tears back.

"So was I," he said still hugging her. "But you know I wasn't ready to check out of here. I got too many things to handle and take care of, including you."

Me and Lynda stepped out of the room to give Ricardo and Kyle time to talk. They were only going to keep him there overnight but we stayed up there until visiting hours were over. He was fortunate to have only been hit in the arm and the leg and both bullets had gone in and out.

It was a relief watching him laugh and joke with my mom but I knew from Kyle's demeanor that things were about to get ugly.

Driving back home, my mother asked if I would still be ok staying at home alone for the next two weeks. Honestly I was a little shook by what had happened but I was looking forward to the freedom. I assured her that I was all good.

Later on that night she poked her head in my room, "You sure you ok?"

"Yea, I'm okay Ma. Go to bed you have to leave early in the morning," I replied genuinely concerned about her. I jumped up and hugged her.

As I closed my eyes I realized that I hadn't talked to Rico in two days, and this was the time I needed him most.

Chapter Three

I felt my mom kiss my forehead around 5:30 that morning, then the next time I was awaken by the sun streaming through the blinds. I called her cell phone to check on her then I called Ricardo's room at the hospital. We talked for a minute and he promised to go home and get some rest when they released him.

I was so relieved that he was ok. Now it was time to enjoy the freedom! Two weeks of nothing but freedom, and fun. The girls were over by noon. I was telling them how I planned to get Rico back on track. We had been close to making love millions of times but I always stopped him before we got into it. I know that it frustrated him and I also knew it was part of the reason I couldn't get in touch with him when I wanted to but after tonight, all that was going to change.

"So tonight is the night, huh?" Jade said as she walked in my room and handed me the phone.

I was going to get in touch with Rico if it killed me. He and I hadn't talked in awhile, but I knew he would be glad to know I was ready to take our relationship to the next level. "Yeah, I'm hoping it is," I said dialing his number.

"If you ask me, I don't think you should. Ya'll barely talk and when ya'll do it's only for a minute 'cause he oh so busy!" Kiyah commented as she combed her hair in my vanity mirror.

"Well I didn't ask you, but maybe this will bring us closer," I said immediately getting on the defensive.

"You don't need to have sex with someone to make them love you, or to feel loved. If ya'll ain't close now, then it's no point of trying. Didn't your father teach you anything?"

They all looked at me after that statement and Kiyah instantly wished she could take it back. She knew my father had never taught me anything. I got up off the bed and walked out of the room.

"Yo, my bad Monnie," she said as I stormed out.

"Damn Kiyah, that was cold," Jade said following behind me. "You good?" she said rubbing my back.

"Oh, yeah I'm good. I know she just be trying to look out." I was used to Kiyah's tough love. That was just how she was, but my mind was made up and it was nobody's decision but mine.

After about three phone calls, I finally got in touch with Rico. He was coming over tonight and I was more than ready. We spent the rest of the day watching videos and snacking. I waited patiently for Rico to show up. At nine thirty the doorbell rang.

"I still don't think he deserves to be your first," Kiyah said not letting up on me.

"Okay, well I do. Now can you leave me alone?" I rushed to the door when I heard the door bell ring again.

"Hey Boo," I said giving him a big hug.

"Hey, how ya'll doing?" he spoke as he came in the door noticing the girls there.

Reality

Rico was so handsome. He stood there all five feet seven inches of him with all black on. Something about all black turned me on. He was caramel with a little facial hair trying to come in.

After the girls spoke to him I immediately got down to business. "Let's go upstairs," I suggested as I grabbed his hand and pulled him towards the stairs. I saw Kiyah rolling her eyes and Jade playfully pushing her shoulder out the corner of my eye.

"So what's been up Rico? I haven't talked to you in days. That's how we are now?" I sat down next to him, trying to let him know how he had been making me feel.

"Nothing, just grinding. I have been thinking about you though. You know we straight, babygirl."

That simple statement gave me hope that I was still in his heart and on his mind. "You sure don't pick up the phone to tell me that, or answer when I call," I said waiting to hear his comeback.

"I'm working. I told you from day one this is how it was going to be." Rico was right I knew what type of guy he was from the start so it wasn't no changing that.

"You right, my bad. I just wish we could spend more time together, do things together."

I kind of hated that I ended up falling for a guy who was all into the streets; because I felt I never stood a chance. A lot came with being a street nigga, money, cars and girls. The fast life always came to a fast end.

"We will, just chill Monnie. I'm getting my car next week so we can start doing things together then."

I smiled after that, I believed everything this boy told me. "For real?"

"Yeah," he said leaning against me starting to kiss me.

My body was feeling things I had never felt before, it was this tingly feeling. I was feeling weak and very vulnerable. I start moving my body with same motion as his. Before I knew it he was removing my clothes, and I was tugging at his. "Ahh…" I moaned as he kissed me passionately all over my neck.

He eased me back onto the bed, and I didn't hesitate. I was ready for it all. He stood up and took off his shirt and pants, leaving nothing but his boxers on.

"Baby, I love you," I whispered as he was climbing on top of me.

"I love you too, Ar'monnie," he absently replied. His focus was getting the rest of my clothes off.

As much as I knew Kiyah was right I didn't want to believe it. I was so caught up in it with this boy, it felt as if nothing else mattered but him.

He slowly rubbed his hands over my body. I felt so comfortable with him. I felt his manhood rise against my thigh. I touched it and almost went crazy. He put his hands in my panties, and pulled them off. I could feel the moistness between my legs, and now he was feeling it.

Reality

"That feel so good," I moaned out as he rubbed my spot and used his fingers slowly to open me up.

"I want the real thing," I moaned pushing him off me so he could take off his boxers. He looked a little surprised at my forwardness but his touch had sent me over the edge. He took his boxers off and reached in his pants pocket for the condom. I watched him eagerly as he rolled the latex on.

I would soon find out the pleasure would be short-lived. When he entered my body it felt as if I had just been ran over by a semi truck. "Rico!" I screamed as he pushed and pumped until he was all the way in. For the next fifteen minutes I was in hell. When he came I was so happy, my pussy was pounding and I could barely move. Sex was nothing like I thought it would be. I prayed the next time it would be better.

"You okay?" he asked while putting his clothes on.

"Yeah," I lied. My insides were on fire and I my legs were weak. My heart was also hurting as I quickly saw that there would be no cuddling. He barely acknowledged that I was still laying there when he sat on the edge of the bed to put his shoes on.

He stood up and asked me, "You gon' walk me out?"

"Yeah," I said slowly rising from my bed of pain. I put on some shorts and a tank top and walked him to the door. We kissed bye, and I was left to tell my girls all the horrid details. Of course I switched the whole story up. They knew of a fairy tale 'first-time' and the real truth was something that only Rico and I would ever know. They didn't need to know all my business, not the bad stuff anyway. That night I lost something that I had held on to for seventeen years, not only my virginity but I would slowly see my pride as well.

Chapter Four

I spent the next two weeks learning the ins and outs of having sex with Rico and making sure that he wasn't around when my cousins came to check on me. The days belonged to my girls but the nights belonged to Rico. He started buying me gifts and we went out a few times after he got his Mustang.

Once my mom came back things slowed down tremendously. There wasn't an open bed anymore and he knew that. Everyone started to see the change in him, except me I was blinded by nostalgia of the sex and all the gifts. What I thought was gold was still glittering to me.

My cousins began to see a change in me, and it's nothing like the people you look up to; looking down at you.

He started the old routine of not answering his phone or shooting me to voicemail until he was ready to talk. But as soon as he called I was there, ready and waiting. I could feel myself being a sucker for his love, and I kind of knew where this love was going to end up but I was too far gone to turn back.

One Friday after Lynda had gone to work, like always Rico slid through. Normally we would get a quickie in and he would be gone, but today was different. While I was getting out of the shower, Rico was sitting on my bed on the phone.

"Man, come on through!" I heard Deon say loud as ever. Deon was one of Rico closest friends; it was always three of them. Antonio, Deon, and Rico.

"Alright man, I'm waiting for Monnie to get dress then we'll be there," he said before he hung up.

"Where we going?" I asked drying myself off.

"Just get dressed."

Even though sometimes it seemed harsh, I loved the way he took control. It made me feel special. I didn't know where we were going, maybe he was surprising me. After about ten minutes, I was fully clothed and ready to go.

As we were making our way to the party, Rico was banging 2pac, "Me and My Girlfriend." I listened to the words very carefully and fell in love with the song.

"*Me and my girlfriend must've fell in love with the struggle,*" Rico rapped that part out loud. I felt so safe around him. I knew he had my back the same way I had his.

When we pulled up on Mendota I saw some of everybody, people from the hood and people from school. This was the place to be tonight.

Rico was shaking hands with everyone; getting treated like a king. I had to admit though it was a major turn on.

"I see ya'll out here," Deon said approaching us, as we walked in the house. Everybody was in the living room dancing, smoking and drinking.

"Yeah, I had to have my girl roll with me," Rico grabbed the blunt from Deon and puffed it. I wondered if weed was as relaxing as everybody said it was.

"Let me hit it," I asked timidly, afraid of what Rico would say.

"Here," he passed it to me and seemed happy that I wanted to try it.

After about four hard puffs, I could feel it swelling in my chest. My heart was beating faster than it ever had before.

"You want a drink?" Rico asked while holding on to my waist. I smiled up in answer. A minute later he returned with two drinks, one for him and one for me. I didn't even ask what it was, I trusted him and I knew he would never do anything to hurt me.

"Let's dance," I grabbed Rico's hand and we made our way to the makeshift dance floor. They had moved all of the furniture out of the living room. I was on cloud nine as I was grinding against my Boo. "This is my song," I said waving my hands in the hair while my butt was on his manhood. The DJ was on point playing the Hot Boys "I need a Hot Girl." All eyes were on us and I loved it. I watched as girls rolled their envious eyes.

After we danced we walked outside where it seemed the party had relocated. It was like a car show out there. Everybody who was anybody was out there. I parted away from Rico and started walking around with a girl I knew through Kyle.

"Girl, you too messed up and your cousin is here," Savona said holding on to my arm because I could barely keep my balance.

"Who?" I asked terrified. I knew if either one of them saw me it would be over for me.

"Kyle, but he is on the other end of the block though; so you good."

'What a relief,' I thought to myself. We continued to walk and I was amazed at all the guys that were out here. All of them had money, power and respect and some were fine as hell too.

"What up lil' mama?" said a handsome, light-skinned guy as we walked past him.

"Who?" Savona said wishing it was her that he was talking to.

I kept walking. I didn't think a guy in his right mind would talk to me. They had to be crazy if they knew who my family was and who my boyfriend was.

"She knows who I'm talking to, Lil'Mama in the black."

I turned around and the guard that I had up came falling down as I looked at his beautiful smile. My mind told me to keep walking but my heart wanted to stop. My heart won the battle.

"I can't even talk to you. I'm playing wifey right now," I said blushing.

"Well, I ain't trying to break up no happy home. I just want to get to know you," he said leaning up off the car.

"Girl, go to talk him. It ain't like Rico don't mess with other girls," Savona enlightened me as I was already making my way over to the guy. I made a mental note to question her about that later. We met each other half way. We were standing in the middle of the street like there was nothing to hide.

"How you doing?" he asked looking me up and down.

"I'm fine," I said it all smooth like I wasn't nervous at all.

"That's good, so what's your name?"

"Ar'monnie and yours?"

"It's Dig," he said in a melodic tone that made me weak.

"Dig? What's your real name?" I said putting my hand on my hip, laughing.

"I only tell my close friends my real name," he said smiling down at me, unknowingly casting a spell on me.

"Then consider me a close friend or are you scared to share your government name?' I teased him on two different levels.

He laughed, "Ok, my new close friend it's Dale, but enough with the government name games. Can I get a number or something?"

"No, but I can take yours, and how old are you by the way?"

"I'm twenty-two, is that a problem?" he asked taking my phone from my hand and adding his number to my contacts. I knew he was older than me, but I didn't expect him to be that old.

"Well it might be for you, because I'm only seventeen," I was a little embarrassed to say.

"Damn, you playing! I thought you were at least nineteen or twenty."

"Well you don't have to make me feel bad," I grabbed my phone from his hand turning to walk back to where Savona was standing.

"Naw, you good but call me sometime," he yelled as I walked off.

I would have loved to stay and talk to him, but I knew I couldn't. I blamed my flirting on the alcohol and tried to shake that tingly feeling off. I was with Rico and I loved him. I know he did his dirt, but I was certain that I was still number one in his life.

"Girl…he was fine," Savona said as we started walking back towards the house.

"I know, but what did you mean about Rico talking to other girls."

"Look Monnie, a nigga is going to be a nigga. I know how ya'll is but ain't no nigga faithful. He in the streets and a lot comes with that lifestyle. Always remember a nigga can tell you he loves you from the bottom of his heart, but trust and believe there is room for another bitch at the top," Savona preached.

I knew what she said was true. I thought about my cousins and I knew they never had just one girl. They were in love with the money, sex and the streets. Savona was older than me and had experienced a lot so I could trust what she was saying.

As we approached the house I saw Rico and Deon standing out in front. I noticed three girls walking from that direction, but I didn't think much of it. Savona on the other hand was already peeping game. “You see,” she whispered as she elbowed me to pay attention.

I shook my head. A year ago his ass couldn’t buy a date, now Rico had a fan club. I remember my cousin always telling me that when you’re up, everybody loves you. To me that’s exactly how it was with Rico. Now he had the money, flashy clothes, jewelry and cars; so the girls loved him. Whenever I caught him up in something he would say that the girls did stuff on purpose to mess with my head because they wanted what I had. I believed every word he said.

“Aye, I’m out. Call me later,” Rico said giving Deon some play.

“Alright. You coming back through?” Deon asked as we were walking off.

“Yeah, I have to get her home,” I didn’t realize what time it was. I was having so much fun. I didn’t understand why he just couldn’t stay in too. I was going home so I felt so should he.

“Bye, Savona,” I waved as we walked up to the car. There were a group of girls walking past the car, and as I was leaning down to get in I saw one of them signal Rico to call her. I looked up at his face, and he nodded his head okay. I was more hurt that he was sneaking with a girl right in my face.

“Who was that?” I wanted to hear the lie.

“One of Deon or Antonio’s girls. Chill out Monnie,” he said it as if it didn’t even bother him to lie to me. I kind of knew he was messing around on me, but I didn’t really want to believe it. As much as Kiyah and my cousins stayed trying to kick game to me, it was like Rico’s game worked better.

On the way home, we rode in silence. I looked over at him and it was like he was in a serious thinking mood. When we pulled up in front of my house, he didn't say a word.

"Damn, can I get a hug or a kiss?" I said with an attitude.

He leaned over and kissed me.

"I love you, Rico."

"Love you too," he leaned back in his seat; as I was opening the car door.

When I opened the door, the light came on and beamed directly on a passion mark on his neck. It felt as if a ton of bricks had fallen on my heart. I wanted to jump in his seat and beat the crap out of him. I felt so stupid and worthless. My self-esteem went from a ten straight to a zero.

"Alright, I'll call you," he said rushing me out of the car. I obviously wasn't moving fast enough for him. I was sitting there stuck staring at the mark. I got out, and put all my force into closing his door. I wanted to tear it off the hinges. He didn't even wait for me to get in the house before he was tearing off down the street.

I walked in, and to my surprise the first face I saw was Ricardo's. He had been staying over a few nights a week since he got out the hospital. I was usually good about clocking him so I'd get here before he did, hadn't worked tonight though.

"I'm not even about to say nothing. Hurry up and go change before your Mama pulls up," he said all in one breath and didn't look at me once. I knew he was disappointed. I would have rather him curse me out or something. For him not to really say anything at all hurt more than any punishment.

I walked upstairs feeling so low, on top of stupid. My night had turned out to be a complete waste. I got in the shower thinking that would help me clear my mind; instead I broke down. 'I try so hard to leave him alone, but I can't. He treats me so bold. All I ever wanted was for him to really love me,' I cried to myself. When I finally got in the bed I was literally exhausted. I was sleep in no time.

Chapter Five

I rolled over on a piece of paper on my pillow, "*We have to talk. Call you on my break, Love Mommy.*"

"Fuck!" I yelled thinking that could only mean one thing, Ricardo had sold me out. I dragged myself out of bed and made my way to the bathroom. I looked in the mirror and my eyes were swollen half way shut from all the crying I'd done.

"Aye, hurry up outta there!" Kyle yelled through the door. He stopped over in the morning to check on me.

"Here I come," I sighed. I splashed some water on my face for good measure. Hopefully the cold water would take some of the swelling out of my eyes. I opened the door and tried my best to brush past him as fast as I could. The last thing I needed was him questioning me.

I walked back in my room, and decided to call Rico. I wasn't surprised when he didn't answer, he rarely ever did. So I called my girl, Kiyah.

"What's up Monnie, baby?" she said joking as she picked up.

"Girl, tell me why…" I started giving her all the gossip. About ten minutes later I was getting a lecture.

"Look girl, like I told you before, don't sit around and wait on him to come around. You don't have to hold him down while he is out doing him. If it was the other way around do you think he would wait on you?"

I sat there quietly because I knew she was right. Everyone always told me he wasn't the one for me, but it was more than that to me. I knew he had it in him to be right and do better. He just needed to grow up.

"I know, but I really think we are meant to be together, just probably not right now. I'm not going to break up with him though, when he's done playing around and running the streets he'll be back home," I assured her, feeling kind of stupid trying to convince myself more than her.

"Well I'm not going to judge you. Just don't let him know that door is always open because then he will come and go as he pleases and you will always end up hurt."

'It was already too late for that,' I thought to myself.

"Just be smart Monnie. Play the game, don't let it play you."

"I hear you. It's crazy how you be schooling me like you are older than me," I laughed but thinking she really was the most mature of all us.

"Because, I have an old soul," she joked. "But I'm going to check on you later. I have something lined up," she said rushing me off the phone.

"Must be one of your Honey Dips?"

Kiyah was a player; she never let her feelings get involved. She just had pure fun. She always said she was too young to be in love. That a real relationship took time and energy she didn't have. I wished I felt that way.

"You know it is. Call me later, love you."

Reality

"Love you more," I said hanging up my line. I sat in my room for a moment and went over last night's events. I smiled when I thought of Dig. There was something about him that I couldn't put my finger on. Everyone knew I was with Rico so most guys wouldn't even approach me, but that hadn't stopped Dig. As much as I wanted to call him, I couldn't bring myself to do it. I loved Rico and I thought calling another guy would be cheating. I felt like I owed Rico something so I made my mind up that I was going to stick it out with him. I loved him and I knew deep down he loved me too.

I got dressed and went downstairs. Ricardo and Kyle were sitting in the living room talking in hushed voices. They stopped talking when I walked in the room. The last thing I heard was, "I heard Rocky been spending money like crazy."

I rolled my eyes at Ricardo and flopped down on the couch next to Kyle. I picked up the remote and changed it to the 'Jerry Springer show.'

"I wish we could just go on here and settle it like that," Ricardo said to Kyle, who laughed and agreed.

"Yeah little bro, I wish it was that easy. I really do."

. "Did your Mom call?" Ricardo turned off the TV and finally looked at her.

"No, I guess she forgot. Why? You ratted me out?" I said with much attitude.

"Naw, you know you was wrong. I shouldn't have to tell you or tell her. I ain't gon' be on yo' head like that but you gotta make the right decisions. Look, I just want you to finish school. I want you to go away to college and live the right way."

I sat there confused. I wasn't sure if someone had seen me at the block party and told them or what. I wasn't sure what angle he was coming from but I knew he was mad about something. The fact that Kyle was sitting there and not saying anything didn't sit well with me either.

"Ok, just because I came in late doesn't mean I'm going to drop out of school."

"I'm not talking about just last night. I'm saying I want you to have the best; and promise me you going to finish school." Ricardo eyes were turning red and his face was flush, I knew he meant business.

"I will. What's wrong with you?" I said looking at him, getting worried. "What's wrong with ya'll?"

"Nothing we can't handle," they said at the same time. "Gon' over your friend's house, we got some shit to talk about," Ricardo said dismissing her.

"Ar'monnie," Kyle called out. "Be careful," he finished as their eyes connected.

"I will," I said walking out the door wondering what was going on with them.

Chapter Six

I spent the rest of the day chilling with the girls and waiting for Rico to call. He never did. I started to blow his phone up but what good would that have done? Like always, he was going to call when he was ready and I was going to be there ready and waiting. It was a sad reality that was beginning to sink in with me. I made sure I was in the house at a decent time so that my mom and cousins wouldn't be tripping. I was back in bed by ten o'clock but the rest of the city was alive and popping.

"Man, why you go buy them damn rims?" Money yelled at his stick-up partner Rocky. Rocky stood on the curb admiring the twenty-six inch rims that he had on his Yukon. He loved the way they were beaming under the street light.

"Nigga, I ain't worried about them mutha fucka's. We on a come up. Them niggas can't have all the shine. That nigga Ricardo had it coming anyway," Rocky replied.

"Rock. Man, them niggas get word that you spending like this, they gon' know it was us that bombed on Ricardo. Nigga, I don't know about you but I ain't ready for that beef," Money explained.

He regretted bringing Rocky in on this job. Hell, he regretted taking it on himself but when the nigga brought it to him, it just seemed too good to be true. Money was a corner boy by trade but he did stickup on small time dealers like himself. He never thought about moving up to the big timers. Rocky was the only nigga he knew that would be willing to ride but the thought of the money blinded Money's judgment when he chose Rocky. Rocky ran around town with a death wish. He fucked with everybody and had a big mouth too.

"Nigga, you ain't told nobody have you?" Money asked Rocky.

"Money, why you so shook? These niggas bleed just like us! And hell naw, I ain' told nobody," Rocky lied knowing just hours ago after he finished sexing his bottom bitch Tiana, that he was pillow talking trying to impress her and had told her all about it. Little did he know that Tiana had been fucking Kyle for years and she couldn't get on the phone quick enough to tell Kyle the scoop.

Money pulled the blunt to his mouth and inhaled hard. He needed something to calm his nerves. He made a call on his cell phone and cursed when the call went straight to voicemail. He had been trying to call this nigga for a week and he wasn't picking up.

"Come on nigga, let's go make it rain at the bar," Rocky said pulling out a knot of money. "You need some big ass slapping on yo' lap so you can calm the fuck down," he said jumping in the truck.

'Maybe, he's right,' Money thought to himself. 'I'm tripping. If them niggas was coming they would have been came.' He hopped in the passenger seat and they headed to Hot Shots on Eight Mile.

As usual the club was packed to capacity with drug dealers, local celebrities and butch bitches all fighting for the strippers attention. Whoever had the most money was winning. Money and Rocky made their way through the club slapping hands with everybody they knew. Rocky caught Tiana's eye as she rolled and grinded on the lap of an unsuspecting gentleman. She smiled and licked her lips. He pretended that it didn't matter but felt the sting in his heart. He knew he couldn't change a hoe into a housewife but if he had to try, it would be with Tiana. He and Money bought a booth and some singles and played with the waitress for a minute. They sat back admiring all the nakedness around them. It wasn't long before two dancers came up to grace them with their presence. The ladies didn't waste any time striking up a conversation and pushing a dance on the men. Rocky accepted his dance and looked around for Tiana, but didn't see her.

After two dances and a promise of some head, the two couples moved to the VIP room for some 'privacy.' The girls led them over to a couch and proceeded to pleasure them. Both men laid back and let the weight of the world float off their shoulders.

Tiana pointed to the VIP room and Kyle nodded as he helped Ricardo who was on crutches to the bar. The two thugs that were with them headed to the door of the VIP room, one slipped the bouncer who stood at the door a wad of money and he turned his head as the two men walked in. The two ladies hurriedly walked out of the room and sought out another lap to grind on. A few minutes later gunfire erupted in the tightly packed club.

Chaos ensued immediately. Everyone was headed for the doors. Scantily clad women ran for safety as the men in the club pushed to the door or took cover. Kyle and Ricardo moved to the side of the bar waiting to see that the job that they had ordered had been completed. They couldn't have been more surprised to see Rocky running out of the VIP room with his guns brandished.

Ricardo immediately jumped into action pulling the Glock he had hid in his sling out and dumping three bullets into Rocky's body. Kyle stood over him and finished the job by giving him one in the head and one in the heart. The two men exited the building the same way they had come in. Outside the club they could hear the sirens coming. They got into their car the same way everyone else who had been inside were scrambling to do.

Inside the bar, the dancer known as "Barbie" climbed out from under a table shaking like a leaf. With her hand covering her mouth she stepped over the dead body and hurried out of the bar, bumping right into the first police officer on the scene.

Money's bloodied corpse lay slumped on the couch. His face wore the look of regret. The two thugs that Rocky had managed to shoot lay a foot away from Money, one dead and the others life slowly leaving his body.

Chapter Seven

The next day I woke up, stretching in my bed. I did the usual routine of checking my phone, no missed calls. This was really starting to bug me. He hardly ever called me and when I called him he never answered. I was beginning to figure I was wasting my time with him. I threw the phone on the bed and went into the bathroom to wash my face and brush my teeth. I heard Lynda downstairs getting ready to leave for work.

I figured she must have just forgotten about wanting to talk to me and that was fine by me. I didn't need another lecture. I ran downstairs to give her a hug before she left.

Ricardo was laid out on the couch snoring loudly as I ran past the room to catch my mom. I caught her just as she was about to open the door, but we both were surprised when the door came crashing down. There were red and blue flashing lights in front of our house and a trail of policemen were making their way through the door. At least three cars rolled up and the sirens were indicative that more were on the way. One of the officers yelled out, "We have a warrant."

"Aww shit!" Ricardo yelled trying to get up off the couch.

Lynda had fallen to the ground from the impact but she was up and running towards them quicker than she'd fallen.

"Get down! Don't move!" they screamed as one of the officers roughly grabbed her and forced her to the ground. I was ordered to do the same by a female officer.

"No, Ricardo!" I cried out as I saw them charging towards him. "Let him go!" I got up making my way towards him, but the lady police officer was holding me back.

Lynda got up off the floor and was grabbing me.

"What did he do?" Lynda asked as they were cuffing him and reading him his rights.

"He knows why we're here," one of the officers said.

"I love you lil'girl," he said staring at me.

"I love you too," I cried trying to shake my way out of Lynda's arms to hug him. My whole world seemed to shatter right before my eyes. I didn't know what to think. I felt so much of me had just died and I didn't know what to do.

"I love ya'll. Don't worry about me," is all he kept saying as they took him out.

"No…" I cried harder and louder as they took him out the house. Once they put him back of the police car, I ran in the kitchen and called Kyle but he didn't answer.

After they were gone one of our neighbors came and helped my mom put the door back on. Lynda had planned on calling in to work and going down to the station but Ricardo's attorney had already called and said it wasn't necessary for us to come down there. Ricardo wasn't going anywhere, any time soon.

Chapter Eight

The next day was such a drag. Everyone was calling to check on me but I knew they were just being nosey. I picked up and called Kyle again and there was still no answer.

"Ma, have you talked to Kyle?" I asked walking down stairs finding her sitting at the dining room table.

"Yes, he was picked up last night too, Monnie," she said looking up at me. It took a minute to register in my mind exactly what she was saying. I started backing up, until I couldn't back up anymore. I was leaning on the wall and I slid down crying into my hands.

"Monnie, it's going to be alright. Stop crying, baby," she tried lifting me up, but I wouldn't move.

"No it's not! They both are in jail, Mama!" This was like a nightmare that I couldn't wake up from. It felt like someone had put a hex on me.

"I need you to be strong until we really know what's going on. They wouldn't want you crying." Lynda wiped my face, as I lifted my head up. "Come on upstairs with me for a minute," she said pulling me up to my feet. When we got to her bedroom she reached on to the shelf in her closet and pulled down a black box. From that she pulled out a beautiful bound book.

"What book is that Mama?" I asked through my tears.

"This is a journal that your Grandmother gave me before she passed away. She wrote it in every day and then I started writing in it whenever I was feeling down or going through something," she said flipping through the pages. I knew that the book meant a lot to her and was surprised as she passed to me.

I flipped through the pages and noticed Kyle's handwriting in the journal as well. She explained, "Kyle started writing in it years ago, too."

I was even more honored to be the next recipient of a book that was slowly making its way through the generations in my family. I wasn't a writer but it meant a lot anyway. We sat there for a minute in deep thought.

I was determined to make things right. I wanted my cousins back home. I needed them in my life. They were the closest things to a father that I had and they meant the world to me.

I went in my room and made a phone call. I was surprised to hear a real voice rather than an automated one. "Rico, why haven't you been answering your phone?" I said when he picked up.

"Chill, I lost my phone. You straight? I heard about your cousins," he asked as if he truly cared.

"How you know?"

"Man, that shit all over the hood. I heard they gave it to the nigga that shot Ricardo up."

I didn't know myself what was going on, but I knew the hood did. "I don't know what happened, but we are going to court on Monday. When can I see you?" I asked, he would come over to talk with me. I needed some support.

"Well I got something lined up tonight, but I can stop by tomorrow."

I knew not to believe him, but my heart wanted to, "Okay."

We hung up, and I was left to think. What if my cousins don't come home? My birthday was next week, and they wouldn't be here. What about when I start school, they are not going to be here. My prom and graduation, they are going to miss. The day I go away to college; they are not going to be here. This was going to be harder than I thought.

My cell phone rang and "Private Caller" came across the screen. I figured it must be Ricardo or Kyle. I quickly scrambled to answer it.

I was surprised when I heard a child's voice ask to speak to me.

"Yes, who is this?" I asked trying to figure this out.

"Hold on," the girl said. I could hear her passing the phone to someone else. I was really getting pissed off. I wasn't in the mood for the games.

"How you doing?" a deep voice came through my receiver.

"Who is this?" I was getting so mad.

"This is Dig. How are you?"

"I'm straight, but how did you get my number?"

"I think you should know by now I get everything I want," he said like he was over there grinning.

"So who was that little girl? Can you answer that question?"

"My little sister, I didn't want to start no drama for you just in case you had somebody else answering your phone," he explained.

"Well, thanks for saving me the drama, but one, no one else should be answering my phone and two, I'm kind of dealing with a lot right now so can I call you later?"

"Yeah, I know all about that. I was calling to see if you wanted to get away and talk about it."

He was being so sweet, it made it really hard to do the right thing and tell him no. I couldn't bring myself to do that. Unfortunately he was stepping in doing the exact thing that I wanted Rico to do. "Sure. Where are we going?" I really didn't care. I just needed someone to be here for me.

"Just get ready."

"Alright, I live on…"

"I know where you stay. I told you I did my research on you," he said laughing.

"Alright, see you in a minute," I smiled into the phone. I got myself together, and was flat ironing my hair when Lynda walked in my room.

"What's wrong with you?" I saw the look on her face and it said trouble. It was always something going on in this family now.

Reality

"I just lost my job," she said sitting on my bed picking up the black box she had given me.

"Why, what happened?" I asked still combing through my hair. I didn't worry much because I thought we still had a lot of money put up from when my Grandma died.

"I told them I couldn't come up there again for two weeks. I have to be here for the boys; they go to court Monday." She wasn't even crying, but I knew she was mad.

"Well, we have money put up and you know Kyle and Ricardo will look out, Ma."

I was worried but I tried to hold it together for her. I had a feeling things were about to get worse before they got better.

"Kyle and Ricardo might be about to do some real time and that money is put up for you to go away to college," she was raising her voice and standing up.

"Okay, but Ma it will be alright. I promise," I hugged her before she walked out my room. I knew deep down she was hurting just like me. I pulled the journal out and I opened to the last page and the title read *Reality*. I started to read it, but I put it down and started to think. I wouldn't even let myself cry, I was getting tired of that. It was time for me to do something about it.

Chapter Nine

I heard Dig's music outside of my house so I grabbed my phone and headed to the door. I told Lynda I was going out with the girls, and I would be home later.

"Hey," I said getting into his truck. He turned down the music, took his hat off and waited for me to get settled.

"How you feeling?" he asked reaching over and hugging me. Something about his hug made me feel special, loved even. I felt secure in his arms and that was something new to me.

"I'm okay," I said leaning back in my seat. I was nervous because I had never been out with a guy other than Rico. But I felt good about this. We hit the Southfield freeway and about fifteen minutes later; we were pulling up to the Holiday Inn.

He held all doors open for me, and I was really impressed. Chivalry was completely new to me. We made our way up to room 305. When I walked in everything looked so comfy. I sat down at the little table that was by the window; and he sat on the bed.

"Here," he threw me the remote. I turned the television on and surfed through the channels until I hit the video channel. 'Promise' the Jagged Edge video was on. I loved this song, it reminded me so much of Rico and all the promises that he had made to me.

"So tell me what's going on with you," he said kicking his feet up on the bed.

The fact that we were at a hotel made me a little uncomfortable but I was so happy to get away from all the drama that I began to relax.

"It's a lot of stuff. Too much to even get into," I said brushing a stray piece of hair from my face.

He got up from the bed and pulled me over to him. "Tell me what's wrong. I brought you here to talk so you can clear your mind. You can talk to me."

"This must be your spot, huh?" I said to change the subject again. I already knew this was a spot that he frequented because the front desk clerk knew him by name!

"Yeah, I come here all the time to get a piece of mind," he said lying back on the bed.

"I see," I said sitting next to him, trying not to get too close. "Or a piece of ass," I thought to myself.

"So tell me why you been crying, your eyes are red."

As much as I wanted to keep him out of my family business, he seemed so inviting. There was something telling me that I could trust him. The wall that I had tried to build was slowly crumbling down. He assured me again that he was here for me. I laid my head on his chest.

"You really just want to listen to my problems?" I looked up at him. He was so handsome and I knew he had to have a bunch of women, I wondered why he was bothering with me and all my drama.

"Not just to hear your problems, but to be there for you," he said leaning up a little so he could see my face better.

I knew he meant well by what he was saying, so I chose to follow my first mind and let it all out. He laid there in silence and listened to every problem I had. Not once did he judge me or my family. He rubbed my back as I talked to assure me that it was okay, and if it wasn't now it would be.

After about two hours, I realized I had to get home. I still had issues to deal with. I had talked so much I was silent on the way back to my house, just listening to the music and thinking.

"I really enjoyed your company Lil' Mama," Dig said turning the music down as I was getting out the car.

"Same here, you're a good listener," I said blushing reaching over to hug him goodbye. I couldn't help wondering what else he was good at.

"I told you, I'm here if you need anything okay?"

I smiled and closed the door. Emotions that I shouldn't have been feeling were being stirred up, considering the baggage that I had. Rico was still in my life to a degree.

I stood on the porch until I saw his truck turn the corner. "Back to Problem Central," I thought to myself as I put my key in the door.

Chapter Ten

I walked in and called out for my mother but got no response. I walked in her room, and the lights were out. I fumbled over to her night stand to turn on her lamp and tripped over something on the floor. When I hit the switch I saw my mother lying on the floor!

I shook her trying to wake her, but she was unresponsive. There was an empty bottle of Tylenol 3's next to her body. I checked her pulse and was lucky enough to find one, though it was extremely faint. I was starting to panic as I dialed 911 and told them what I thought had happened and gave them address. I walked back over to her, and held her face in my lap. I cried and kissed her as I prayed that the ambulance would get here soon enough. I wanted nothing more but for her to survive. I felt like this was all my fault, I should have just stayed home. I knew she needed me.

"Mama, I'm nothing without you. Please don't leave me. I'll do anything. I will take care of you Mama, please. I don't have the courage to go on without you. Please wake up, just hang in there Mama."

When the ambulance arrived I raced to the front door. "She's upstairs," I pointed them in the direction and followed behind them.

In the back of the truck, I held her hand while they went to work. 'I can't handle this. Please Mama, don't do this to me. First my cousins now this, I really can't handle this," I thought to myself as I watched the paramedic take my mother's vitals. I had so much that I wanted for her, for myself and all I needed was for her to live.

We arrived at Sinai Grace Hospital and they took her in through emergency. That was when I realized that I had no one to call. All of our family lived out of state; it was always just me, Lynda and my cousins. I decided to call Kiyah and Rico. Rico didn't answer, and Kiyah answered and was on her way. I sat in the waiting room and waited for her to get there.

"Excuse me is there any family you can call?" the nurse asked standing in front of me.

"I don't..."

"I'm her family, "Kiyah said as she walked up to us. I nearly jumped into her arms. I had never needed someone like I did then.

"Is my mother okay?" I asked looking over at the nurse as Kiyah rubbed my back.

"Yes, we've pumped her stomach but there is a process she must go through before we let her out. Is there any adult that can look after you tonight?" she asked placing her hand on my shoulder.

"No, and I will be staying with my mother tonight," I said adamantly, wiping my face off.

"Okay, you can wait here until the doctor's are completely finished."

I shook my head to let her know I understood and sat back down holding on to Kiyah's hand. Fifteen minutes later the doctor came out, and I was able to go in. I walked up to the bed and she was resting, but I believed she could hear me.

"Mama, this is your baby girl. I'm going to take care of you. I promise I am. I'm going to treat you like the queen you are. I love you," I kissed her on the forehead and placed my head on the edge of the bed.

Kiyah walked in and stood in the door way. "Monnie you want me to stay?" she asked walking closer to me.

"No, you can go. Thank you for coming Kiyah. I will call you tomorrow."

After a second thought she said, "I'm not leaving you up here by yourself." She sat down in the other chair in the room, and listened as I cried and talked to my mother. An hour later, we both were sleep.

I was stirred awake by a low whisper of someone calling my name. She was still tired and weak but my mom was awake. I couldn't have been happier.

"Hey Ma," I leaned up in my chair and placed my hand on top of hers. I was so happy to see her up and talking.

"I'm sorry baby," she whispered starting to cough.

"Don't worry Ma. I'm going to take care of you. I promise," I meant that with every bone in my body. She was going to be alright.

"I have to get out of here, the boys go to court Monday," she pulled back the cover trying to get out of bed.

"No, you have to get better first and talk to some people," I said pulling the cover back over her legs. I wanted to make sure she had a successful recovery. I was going to handle things from here on out, but I needed her to be healthy and alive.

We spent the rest of the morning talking while Kiyah slept most of the morning. Around noon, Jade and Kristin walked in with flowers and balloons.

"Aww...Monnie how's she doing?" Jade asked walking out into the hallway with me to get some water.

"She's doing much better. Thank you for coming," I said hugging her and Kristin.

"I called you both last night when I called Kiyah, but I guess you both were out," I said lying. I didn't want them to feel bad that I hadn't called them.

"Well you know me," Jade laughed. "I was over my cousin's house chilling."

Kristin just said that was ok. She was probably at home studying or something. Kristin never had anything exciting going on in her life, she was a good girl.

"Well I have some news myself but I will tell you all once Kiyah comes out." I was blushing thinking about my night with Dig.

"She needs to hurry up," Jade said mouth wide open wanting to know it all. " I got some news for ya'll too."

Kiyah walked out of the restroom and joined the rest of us in the hallway. I didn't leave out any details.

“I mean for him to take his hat off was something new, I was thinking he was kinda lame for that,” I said frowning my face up.

“No, that’s a real man. My grandma said back in the day that’s how men were, respectful and had manners,” Jade said assuring me that I should appreciate the chivalry that Dig had displayed.

“That’s right Jade, Monnie’s just used to guys being stuck with this hood mentality. You need to grow up and look for the guy who wears his pants up above his butt. You know the one who holds doors open for you and takes the time to listen to you,” Kiyah went on and on.

“I’m not saying anything is wrong with it, but Rico never does those things; so it was just new to me. I was just shocked but it made me feel special,” I said looking at the floor smiling.

“Good, because now you see the difference between a boy and a man,” Kiyah said rolling her eyes to the sky. She couldn’t stand Rico and it showed.

We all sat around and talked for awhile then the girls left and I was alone with my mother. We had spent so much time talking about me that I hadn’t gotten a chance to hear Jade’s news. Lynda was sleeping peacefully so I decided to get a short nap while I could.

Chapter Eleven

The hospital released my mom Sunday morning and we spent the whole day in the house watching television and talking. Lynda kept apologizing for ‘putting me through’ the whole ordeal. I told her that I understood that she was under an extreme amount of stress but I wished that she had talked to me instead of doing what she’d done. It seemed like she was back to her old self; but I wasn’t falling for it. I kept my eyes on her. The doctor had suggested she see a therapist once a week and to get more rest.

I had a lot on my mind as well. I was still sad that my cousins were gone but I also knew that I had to contribute to the household now that Lynda had lost her job. I had to come up with something and fast.

Monday morning I was shocked when Lynda said I couldn’t go inside the courtroom with her. “Mama, why can’t I come in?” I asked as we pulled in front of the 36th District courthouse.

“I really don’t want you to come in Monnie. I’m not sure you will be able to handle some of the things you may hear,” Lynda said paying for parking

“Mama, they are my cousins and I love them. I need to be there for them like they have always been for me. Please Mama, trust me I can handle it,” I said pleading with her.

She smiled and shook her head. “Come on.”

We had to walk through the metal detector and I had to take my cell phone back to the car. I thought she would take that opportunity to leave me but she was standing there when I got back. She walked through the metal detector and I followed. This time we were all good.

The hallways were jammed packed with people all pleading their innocence, whether they were innocent or not. I saw a lot consulting with attorneys going on outside the courtrooms which I thought was weird. Lynda read the posting on the wall and found my cousins names. We finally found the courtroom where their hearing would be held.

"Come on its room 409," Lynda said turning around and touching my shoulder to get me moving. My heart was beating fast as ever, like I was the one on trial. I didn't know what to think all I knew was my cousin's future was in the hands of twelve strangers. People who would only hear the bad and the ugly and none of the good, about the two men that meant the world to me.

"Wait here," she said walking into the courtroom. I sat down in the lobby. I watched all the other people that were out there. I wondered if they were here for the family against my cousins. I wanted to ask, but I kept quiet. After about an hour, I peeked in because she was supposed to come back out and get me. I didn't see anyone but the judge and a cop standing next to a door which I knew was where they kept the inmates until it was time for their case to be heard.

"Excuse me, Miss," a man said walking on the side of me to go in. As he walked in I couldn't help but notice how attractive he was but I didn't really get to see his face. He walked with purpose and commanded attention when he walked in the room. I peeked my head in more and saw Lynda sitting in the front row wiping her face with a Kleenex. I looked on the other side of the courtroom and saw Kyle and Ricardo. Kyle and I locked eyes as the door was closing. I saw a tear fall from his eye. I let the door close and went back to sit down on the bench. This couldn't be good.

Another hour passed and Lynda finally came out with a distinguished older white man walking behind her.

"What happened?" I jumped up and asked before she could get all the way out the door.

"They're being charged with two counts of first degree murder," she said waiting for my reaction. "Go to the car while I talk to their lawyer," she pushed me in the direction of the elevator.

Once I got to the car, I sat there in disbelief. My emotions ran the full gamut starting with sadness and ending in anger. 'Why would they do this to me? They knew they were doing dumb shit, man. Now I don't have anybody. My mother wants to keep walking around like she's superwoman, when she is crying inside. My cousins are facing a life sentence, so it's all up to me; and I have to make things right,' I thought to myself.

"They are facing twenty years to life for both counts," Lynda said getting in the car. "The prosecutors have an eyewitness. This just doesn't look good for them." I noticed she was crying so I put on my brave face for her.

"Mama, it's going to be okay," was the only thing I could tell her even when I knew it may not be. "Here climb over, I'll drive." I got out and walked around to the driver's side.

On the way home she continued to cry and I felt my heart hardening. I would never get that attached to anything else in my life. I wouldn't let anything or anyone penetrate my heart ever again.

"Aye, Mama let's watch our favorite movie," I said as we walked into the house. I had other plans but I wasn't about to let what happen before happen again. This time I was going to leave her thinking everything is okay.

"I'm really not in the mood," she said walking into her room.

"Please," I whined and it worked.

"Alright Ar'Monnie, get it," she plopped on the bed and kicked her shoes off.

I laid under her like I did when I was younger and we both were all in watching "Sparkle."

"Hey Ma, how do you know when you have met the one?" I leaned up and asked.

"You will know, trust me you will feel it. It will be a feeling no other man has ever given to you," she said looking down at me.

I thought back to my 'date' the other night and smiled. I laid back down and finished watching the movie. The movie was so deep to me. It was very touching. The sister was so beautiful but was destroyed by a man. She thought she was in love and felt it was the best thing because he was a high roller.

'Everything that looks good is not always good for you.' I thought to myself before I dozed off.

Reality

"Crawl to me."

"What?" I said as Rico sat on the edge of the bed.

"Crawl to me," he demanded again. He seemed so serious.

"No," I said laughing. He slapped me across the face and punched me in the stomach.

I was caught off guard and quickly covered up to defend myself from the next blows. "No...Stop Rico! Stop!"

"Ar'monnie! Monnie! Monnie wake up!" Lynda said shaking me to wake me up. "Get up girl! You sweating like a faucet and you was screaming Rico's name, telling him to stop. What's going on? Are you ok?" She asked rubbing my back.

"I'm alright, Ma," I said pushing the cover down. I got up and went to my room. I sat on my bed and went over what I had dreamed. 'What was that about?' I asked myself. It served as a wake-up call. Right then I decided I wasn't about to sit around and wait on a guy to do anything for me. My cousins were gone, and I was determined to maintain my status, and take care of my family.

I was going to work my way to the top. I was on the grind to get mine…

Chapter Twelve

I knew I needed money and the easiest way to get was going to be from a nigga and the only person I knew that was getting those chips effortlessly was Kiyah. I dialed her number anticipating a lecture but I was ready for whatever came my way.

"Hey Kiyah," I said as she picked up. I was in a new mind frame; I was trying to get it all.

"Happy Birthday!" she screamed into the phone.

"Uh…" I was so caught up in everything that was going on I'd forgotten my 18th birthday.

"Girl, don't play! What we doing tonight?" she asked laughing at me.

"Nothing, I got some other things to do. I was calling because I need a guy with money who is not afraid to spend."

I knew she wasn't going to like the sound of this, but I didn't care. I had things to do.

"You serious?"

"Yeah. I mean, with everything going on I have to make sure everything is going to be alright over here. I don't need my Mama stressing, and I don't ever want to need for anything myself," I said hoping she would understand.

"Look Monnie, don't even get caught up in the 'money trap.' Money and sex are two things young girls get exposed to and can't handle all that comes with the two," Kiyah said doing what she does best, kicking knowledge to me.

"Kiyah, I promise I'll be smart. This is all business," I promised her, praying that I would keep that promise to her and myself.

"Alright, I mean I make my money too; but I'm smart about it. Everybody is not built to live certain lifestyles. I mean I'm not telling you to be a gold digger but you know there is nothing wrong with appreciating the finer things in life." Kiyah lived her life on the edge. She was living and that is how I wanted to be. I don't want to just exist, I want to live.

"Now I know this guy named Joe that I could put you on," she said going through her mental rolodex.

"You never messed around with him, have you?" I said cutting her off. We didn't play them games. We shared everything else beside panties and guys.

"No, I messed with his boy, but these dudes are nothing to play with Monnie. They about their bread, and they dangerous so keep it straight business and once school roll around you have to hang it up," she was not letting go of me getting back on track, but I appreciated her caring.

"I'm going to hit him up and let him know you'll be calling but don't forget what I said," she warned.

"I won't. Thank's Kiyah," I said storing his number in my phone.

I got dressed and was ready to head out. I was on a mission. A straight up money mission.

"Birthday Girl…" Lynda sang as I was passing the living room.

"Hey Mama, I'm about to go meet up with the girls," I said making a mental note to call them all so they wouldn't call the house while I was gone.

"Well come see what I got you first."

I walked into the living room and there were two bags, and one pair of shoes. I knew for sure things were tight because I never got just one pair of shoes or just two outfits. I was determined to keep my mom happy, so I hugged and cried fake tears to show her how much I loved the gifts.

"I know it's not what you are used to but…"

"But nothing, it's perfect!" I loved her so much because she always made sure I was smiling and to me, that topped all gifts.

"I have to go, I will be home later," I said walking out the door. I was making my way to the nearest phone booth. I wasn't sure I wanted Joe to have the cell number yet.

"Happy Birthday," Rico said pulling up on the side of me as I was walking across the street.

"Thanks," I said and kept walking. I hadn't talked to him since the night he dropped me off… some relationship.

"Where you on your way to?" he said still riding on the side of me as I walked. "My cousin's house," I said changing my direction towards Ricardo's place.

"I thought both of them were locked up? Oh yeah, sorry to hear about your Mom's too," he said like he really cared.

"So if you knew about everything, why haven't you called?" I stopped dead in my tracks. I was pissed! "Now here you were supposed to be my boyfriend, but yet you couldn't call to see how I or my family was doing?"

"I aint have time. Besides I thought Dig would have been there for you," he smiled and pulled off. I wanted to throw a brick at his car. How in the hell did he know about my time with Dig? The only people who knew were the girls. Then he had the nerve to act like I did something wrong, when he was the one who cheated and lied.

I was so mad that I was at Ricardo's house before I knew it. Even though I hadn't planned on coming here, I figured I could chill there for a minute to get my mind right. I was so mad at Rico. When I got closer to the door, I noticed it was already open. I tip toed my way in and pulled out the only protection I had with me, my blade. Kyle had given me it to me my ninth grade year in high school, and I always carried it on my keys.

As I got closer I heard a voice, a man voice sounding as if he was out of breath like he was having sex. My heart was beating so fast, because I didn't know what to expect. I tiptoed quietly to the bedroom door and listened.

"I'm on top of the world now, baby. Even though them dumb niggas Rocky and Money almost fucked it up. I felt those bullets whizzing past and I just knew I was shot. It was time for me to take over the reins anyway," the guy bragged.

"What you talking about baby? Who are Rocky and Money?" the girl asked.

"Don't worry about it. Just be happy that we on a come up. Now give me some more of that good shit."

I listened as the guy continued to talk. My heart almost stopped when I finally recognized the voice. It was Mack…

"Oh my God!" I said covering my mouth. I replayed what he had said. He knew the guys that were trying to rob Ricardo!

"Kyle and Ricardo didn't know what the fuck hit them. Ricardo is my mans, but he didn't need to reign on top forever. He wasn't feeding me right, man. I been standing beside his ass for too long," he said laughing with whoever was in the room with him.

"Damn, baby," a girl voice followed his.

"I love you," he said planting a kiss on the girl. I wanted to bust in the room, but I had nothing. I was going to get him back.

As I was walking off, I heard the girl talking some more. The voice sounded so familiar but I couldn't put my finger on it. The bed started squeaking again indicating that they had started back having sex.

"You love you some Jade, huh…"

"Hell yeah," he grunted.

I had my back on the wall, tears rolling down my eyes. I was so confused. For one, when the hell had they started fucking and secondly did she know what the hell he had done? I would have never in a million years thought she would betray me or my family like this. I trusted her, and for her to know how much my cousins meant to me only made it hurt even worse. I had to get Mack back and I would get Jade back too if she knew anything about it. I could already taste the sweet taste of revenge.

"To me, one who does wrong must not go unpunished," is what I said to myself running out of the house. I was going to make sure they understood that.

Chapter Thirteen

"Welcome to my neck of the woods," Joe said picking me up from our meeting spot. He wasn't anything like I expected him to be. He was black as midnight, and he was tall as ever; he reminded me of a younger Michael Jordan.

"So what's up Shorty? What's your resume?" he asked looking me up and down. I stood looking up at him, thinking this was it.

"I'm looking to get money and I'm willing to put in work to get it," I said trying my best to seem hard. I was talking to him like I knew the game and of course I didn't. All I knew was what my cousins and Rico talked to me about.

"So you trying to do business with me?" he said pointing to himself laughing. "Look I don't work with girls. Ya'll soft and can't hold ya'll own. I thought we was on some hook up shit," he said laughing and shaking his head.

I cut right into him and went nuts. "Look that's because you ain't never met a girl like me. I'm loyal and I'm a Jones. Ain't no snitching in my blood. I'm going to ride whenever the time comes. If it comes to me eating, I'm down to do whatever. I'm starving just like you."

"Babygirl, you talking a good game but I don't know," he said thinking hard and long. It might be kinda sweet to have a bottom bitch on his team. He looked her over one more time and tried to not pay attention to her hourglass figure.

"Just give me something. I can show you better than I can tell you." I wanted him to trust me, so I knew I had to go in hard. I wanted him to know I wasn't for any games.

"Alright tomorrow meet me here, and then we start." he said walking off to get into his car.

I rushed home, and called Kiyah. I told her what was up, and told her I was going to be with him tomorrow just in case something was to happen. For the rest of the night I chilled, talked to everyone who called to wish me happy birthday and I was out for the night.

The next day, I was dressed in all black, ready to get it in. I must admit I was a bit nervous, sweating like crazy; but I could hear Kyle saying "Never let them see you sweat." I met him at our spot and we got to work.

"Now look you gotta start small. Every nigga out here worked from the bottom up," Joe coached me.

"Yeah I know that, so what I'm working with?" I was ready. I wanted the money.

"You know how to bag right?"

I sat there knowing I didn't but it couldn't be that hard. I was about to learn one way or another, "Yeah," I said with a look that said, "Of course I do."

"I'm pretty sure you know how to drive, right?" he asked looking at me.

"Yep," I said.

"Now I'm trusting you, cause you Kiyah peoples. I know she wouldn't put me down with a snake but I'm all about my business."

"Most def, I understand."

Reality

When we hit the block I took control. I walked in like I owned the place. I grabbed the bags and got to it.

"Damn sweetie, you straight to it, huh?" He said looking over my shoulder as I was sitting at the table putting the drugs in the mini bags.

"I told you I'm all about my business, well about my money," I said not even looking up at him.

"Well I'll pay you $200 for bagging, and if you do drop offs that's another two or three. He said walking out of the house leaving me to work.

For the next two months, it was easy money. I was loving it. I had to stack my change to be able to take care of the people that had betrayed me.

Things at home were straight because I kept money flowing in and that kept my mother at bay. My cousin's both were found guilty and were sentenced to a minimum of fifteen years in prison. I kept to myself and kept Kiyah up on what was going on. Jade, I played especially close. I was still trying to see if she had been in on the set up. She didn't seem shady like that, but she still hadn't told me that she was talking to Mack. I didn't know why she was keeping it a secret. So the verdict was still out on her. I was playing it smart on all levels, except with Rico. I let him dip back into my life and my bed whenever he wanted to. It wasn't love anymore though for me, it was purely casual.

He never brought the Dig situation up again, nor would he even tell me who told him. I honestly know he didn't really care anyways; he was still getting what he wanted out of me so to him it didn't matter who I talked too. I was content with how things were between us, he looked out and gave me money and was still buying me things. Besides, I had my own hustle so I was straight.

Dig and I were still close. He was a friend I called on whenever I felt down and wanted to talk. I believe he wanted to mold me into the girl he wanted me to be. I had nothing against that except I was not that girl. I found my own way of living, and my own way of doing things. It kept the bills paid and kept me fly. I didn't need for anything again and that's how I liked it.

Chapter Fourteen

School was around the corner and I had no plans of going back, I wanted money. That Friday was like any other, I was bagging up and Joe was in the back drinking and smoking; so basically I was running things.

I heard three knocks at the door, and hesitated to go answer it because I never did. Joe would always answer because everyone would call before stopping by. They knocked again, and I made my way to the door. Once I got up I got this feeling in my gut that something wasn't right.

I didn't pay it any mind and thought maybe I was hungry and headed to the door. I looked through the peep hole, and Rico was standing there with two other guys with guns.

I couldn't believe Rico was going to rob the spot! I was in shock. My heart said, 'Open the door' and let him know that I was there. My mind said, 'I couldn't sale Joe out.' I was stuck in the middle and I knew Joe would kill him; but shit they was trying to get in to kill us. It was kill or be killed.

I ran to the back, "Aye Joe, we got static at the door." I was scared as ever. I had never been in a heated situation like this before.

"Straight," he said getting off his bed and grabbing his gun. Before we could get to the door we heard gunshots.

"Ahh..." I screamed jumping next to Joe.

He flipped over the mattress and grabbed three guns. "Here bust!" he said handing me a gun.

"What?" I said with so much fear running through my body. What if Rico and I made a mistake and killed each other? I looked at the gun, and I could hear the gunshots getting closer to the room we were in.

"When I say shoot, shoot Monnie," Joe said taking the safety off his gun. I heard the nigga's standing outside the door. My heart was pounding a mile a minute.

I was scared for my life. I would never forgive myself if I shot Rico. I knew I had to shoot. I had given Joe my word that I could hold shit down, that I could hold my own.

The door knob turned and soon as the door cracked open Joe screamed, "Bust!"

I just let it rip. I don't know if I was hitting them or not but the gun was doing its own thing! As I was shooting I was partially hiding behind Joe. My face and half of my body was behind him! He hit two nigga's and the other was out of sight.

After it got quiet Joe grabbed my hand and we ran out the room. He was trying to open the back window and I was standing right behind him. I heard somebody creeping up on us, so I cocked my gun back and turned around.

"Ar'monnie," Deon said holding his side where he had been shot. Before I could say anything Joe finished him off with a shot to the head.

"You knew them nigga's?" Joe asked as he hopped out the window.

"Naw, I just knew him from middle school," I lied. I didn't want him to think that I had set this up, but I was also sad to see Deon die. I was tearing up, but I held them in. I couldn't believe I had just seen Deon die right in front of me. I was tripping on the fact that I had been in a shoot out and even more that it had been with Rico and his crew.

I jumped down and followed Joe. We ran to his car as fast as we could and pulled off. He was pushing it up Van Dyke. "I can't believe this," was all he kept saying as he was driving.

I was in the passenger seat in my own little world. This was beyond too much for me. I knew a lot came with this lifestyle but this was a little more than I'd expected. I never thought I would shoot at somebody or be shot at. This was a lot to take in. I tried to let it all register as we rode in silence. I thought to myself, 'What would my cousins think if they knew half of the things I was involved in now?'

"Aye, where you getting dropped off at?" Joe said flying on the freeway.

"Just drop me off at the crib," I said trying to sound normal. I was in tears but at the same time proud of myself. I held shit down, in a way I knew my cousins would be proud of, but a lot of disappointment would have come with that too.

Rico would be proud, had it not been him I was shooting at. As we pulled up I looked around and Lynda's car was gone, that gave me time to get myself together.

"See you at eight and keep this to yourself," Joe said before pulling off.

I got in the shower to try to calm my nerves. My hands had finally stopped shaking. I looked at myself in the mirror and wasn't sure if I liked what I saw. I closed the door to the bathroom and almost peed on myself when I saw Dig sitting on my bed.

"What the hell?" I said holding my chest, "What are you doing in here?"

"We need to talk," Dig said getting up off my bed. I wanted to curse him out so bad, but another part of me wanted to know what was so important that he had to sneak into my house.

"Well not here, we need to go somewhere else," I wouldn't dare let Lynda catch him in here with me.

"Come on," he walked out my room and walked towards the back door.

"So that's how you got in," I said as he was repairing our door, making a mental note to change that door to a more secure one.

"You already know how I get down."

We walked around the corner to where he had parked his car so I wouldn't see it, when I came home. We made our way to his getaway spot, room 305 this time.

"I should have known," were the first words that came out my mouth as we walked in.

"Come on Lil'Mama," he said holding the door open for me.

Up in the room he wasted no time, he got right to it. "So man you just going to mess up your whole future, huh?" he asked standing up in front of me as I sat on the bed.

"I don't know what you talking about," in the most nonchalant voice I could muster up.

"Monnie, on some real shit, you don't see how much you are hurting the people around you? How do you think your Mama is feeling while you run the streets? You think she don't know what you doing? You know the word on the streets is heard in the prisons too, right? Your cousins know what time it is too. School is starting soon, what you going to do about that?"

"First off, you don't know shit about what I do. I'm not hurting anybody. I'm taking care of me and my family, so my mama is all good. As far as my cousins, well they shouldn't have left me out here. They knew I needed them, and they didn't care. They left me to figure out this life stuff on my own. I'm not going back to school right now. I'm too deep in this right now. School is not going to get me the money I need right now."

I listened to myself as I was talking and I didn't feel any remorse. I hated my cousins at times, because if they were out here I knew deep in heart, my life wouldn't have turned out like this.

"Do you hear yourself? You have the opportunity to do and be anything you want to be. You are choosing to live this lifestyle. You are on the road to destruction Ar'Monnie. Don't no real man want his woman out in the streets. You need to get your shit together and get back in school," he preached.

We sat there in silence for a minute not looking at each other. He kept tapping his foot and shaking his head. I could tell he was mad but I didn't care because I had a lot on my mind and what he was talking about didn't mean shit to me at the moment.

"Can you take me back where you got me from?" I asked looking down at the floor.

"Yeah, but just promise me this; you're going to finish school no matter what."

I remembered my promise to Ricardo and that broke me. I let the tears fall and he tried to wipe them from my face.

"Don't touch me!" I said snatching back as he reached for my face. I wanted to promise him but I wasn't sure if I could keep it.

He grabbed his keys, and I was finally on my way home. The ride home we didn't say two words to each other. As I was getting out the car, he stopped me and said "If you drive fast you will crash, don't rush anything. You will get too much a little too soon, and be left high and dry not knowing which way to go."

"Yeah alright," I slammed the door and was thinking about my next move before I hit the stairs to my house.

Chapter Fifteen

I was happy that Lynda was still out. My phone was ringing and I was shocked to see Rico's name and number on the screen. I was afraid to answer. He could be calling because he had seen me at the house.

"What to do?" I yelled out debating.

"Get the phone," Lynda said coming through the front door.

"I was about to," I lied as I picked it up.

"Hello?" I said scared as hell.

"Monnie…he gone man, he gone," he was crying hysterically and I felt terrible because part of it was my fault.

"Who? Who is gone Rico?" I asked acting like I was none the wiser.

"Deon! Man, I need you. Can I see you?"

'So finally Rico needed me, huh? This had to honestly be some kind of joke. All the times I'd cried because I needed him, and he wouldn't even answer his damn phone. He would even know things were not right with me, but yet he never called and…now he need me. Yeah, right!' I thought to myself.

"Well I'm a little busy, but I'm sorry to hear about Deon." Finally I could taste it, the sweet taste of revenge rolled off my tongue when I said it. Karma has a way of coming back and biting you in the ass.

"Huh?" he said obviously surprised at my response.

"I'm busy, but call me tomorrow or something. Love you. Be safe out there," and I hung up. I was not about to be a fool for him anymore. I felt horrible about Deon especially knowing I witnessed it; but life goes on.

"What's wrong with Rico? What happened?" Lynda asked entering the living room as I hung up. She was so nosey.

"His friend died, Ma. Dang you so nosey," I said walking past her heading to my room

"And you can't be there for him?" she said stopping me in my tracks.

"I mean…well no. He wasn't ever there for me when I needed him. When you were in the hospital, when Ricardo and Kyle went to jail, period…so now he sees how it feels," I said walking around her.

"Monnie, you must learn to forgive and forget. The sooner you learn that, the better off you'll be," she said pointing her finger in my face.

"Ma, you the one that said I didn't need to be messing with him anyway."

"Yeah I did, but I also raised you to be generous and respect people feelings. He may not have anyone else to call or talk to. So what if he treated you wrong, you should kill him with kindness. I don't know what has gotten into you but you need to change and fast. Now you've turned your back on him, you may need him before he needs you again." She walked off into the kitchen and I walked up to my room.

I closed my door and tried to shut out the things that she had said. My mother was right about one thing, she had instilled in me morals and values and it seemed like none of that even mattered to me anymore. I didn't care about shit. I lost my heart the day my cousins left; and my soul was gone the day I witnessed my mother cry.

I never thought in a million years I would be like I am, but I loved it. I thought back to what Lynda said about Rico and laughed. "I'm not going to need him, he was never there anyway to comfort me, or even be a friend nonetheless a boyfriend."

I got off the bed and looked at the clock and it was six o'clock. I had to get ready to meet up with Joe. 'Back to the money,' I thought as I entered the shower.

I had turned into a cold hearted bitch over night and I felt the change and wouldn't even stop it. I didn't even recognize the person I had become.

"You busy, huh?" Rico hung up the phone at a loss for words. Never in his lifetime did he think, Ar'monnie would turn her back on him. 'Before she wouldn't even breathe without me saying it was okay to do so,' he thought getting off his bed.

"I can't believe this shit," he said hitting the wall. "I just lost my best friend! I'm definitely getting at Joe. He has to pay. Ar'monnie too and I know just how to hit her heart."

He looked at his phone and starting dialing, waiting for a response. He laughed because he knew how this situation was going to end.

"Hello, Kristin can you come out? I really need someone to talk to. Deon just got killed" he said knowing she would be happy to oblige.

Chapter Sixteen

Even though I'd had a horrible start to my day, I felt better once I took a nap and put on some clothes. I was wearing my hair down and couldn't wait to feel it blowing in the wind.

I flipped my mattress over and took out a thousand dollars. I placed it in my purse and hoped Lynda wouldn't put up a fight and would just take it.

"Mama," I walked in her room and called out. I saw she was sleeping so I opened up her Bible and placed the money in the back of the 'good book.'

I knew she would be surprised when she found it. I had been strategic in the way that I funneled money into the household. I had taken to going directly into DTE or to the water company and just putting money on the bills. She barely paid attention to the balances so when she sent money in, we ended up with credits. I knew she probably wouldn't have taken the money from me. She would always say I was the child and she was the parent. I respected her for that, but she took care of me for so long; now I felt it was time I took care of her.

I heard music outside and knew it had to be Joe, so I flew down the stairs and was out the front door. While riding in the car with Joe I was scared to ask what was his next move was. I knew that he was going to get to the bottom of whoever it was that had tried to rob him.

"So where we going?" I asked.

"Just ride. It's a special treat for you," he was smiling and I didn't know what to think.

"What you up to?" I was dying to know. My stomach was filled with butterflies.

"Just ride baby, you do any other time," he was trying to be smart and choked on his blunt laughing.

"I hate surprises." I leaned back in my seat and decided to not keep asking.

"Well you'll love this one." He looked over at me and touched my shoulder.

After ten minutes of guessing what it could be, we were finally pulling up to one of Detroit's nicer hotels, the Westin. I thought maybe we were just here for a drop off, but I was really in for a surprise when he said, "Did you bring some clothes with you?" he asked parking in front of the door, so the valet could park his car.

"No, I didn't think I needed any," I said confused.

"Good, come on," he helped me out the car. When we walked in everything was so beautiful and elegant.

"I have a reservation under the name Joseph Sanders," he said pulling out his license.

I laughed in my head at his real name.

"Yes sir, we have you right here," the man behind the desk said giving him back his license. "Your guest will be up soon as you are settled."

"Okay, thank you," he said grabbing my hand as we made our way to the elevators.

"What guest?" I asked wondering who the hell he had coming up here.

"Man, be patient! You will fuck a nigga's shit up, asking too many questions," he said jokingly.

He pulled me closer to his chest as we rode up in the elevator. I was feeling kind of uncomfortable because we had never been intimate like this. It was like we were just homies and now he was pulling and touching on me.

When we stepped off the elevator I was like a kid on Christmas, I was so impressed by it all. I walked down the hall with my mouth open wide.

"This is so beautiful," I said holding onto Joe covering my mouth with my other hand.

"Yeah, this is nice."

I had never been to a hotel this nice unless I was with Lynda or my cousins. He opened the door and I could have just died! The bed had white rose petals on it and candles were lit everywhere. There were two glasses of wine on a round table in the sitting room.

"Oh my God! All this for me? I must be employee of the month?" I turned around and faced him.

"No, but you can be my girl."

I paused and looked at the floor. I had never been with anyone except Rico, and that relationship made me never want another one. I also thought of what Kiyah told me, "Keep it straight business," but I thought this wasn't an offer I could afford to pass up. Joe had it all, the money, power and respect.

To be his first lady meant I would be good. I decided to look at it like a business deal.

"Are you serious?" I asked snuggling closer into his chest and peering up at him with my doe eyes.

"Yeah, you know I am. You showed me today that you down and loyal. What more could a street nigga ask for and you beautiful," he stated then kissed me.

There was a knock at the door and Joe let an older white lady in the room. She was carrying a briefcase.

"Hello, Mr. Sanders," she shook his hand before taking a seat.

"Baby, this is my jeweler."

I extended my hand to her, and said "Hello."

"I want you to pick out whatever you want." He grabbed me by the waist and walked behind me over to the table where the lady had the jewelry from the briefcase on display.

"Okay," I said thinking 'I'm loving this business deal already.' I made sure I got the most expensive pieces, so if I had to, I could pawn it. Forget this jewelry I wanted the money! Lynda had bills, and I had a status to maintain.

"So this is all you want, Sweetie?" Joe said touching my face.

"Yeah, I'm good," I said picking up my two bracelets, a necklace, a pair of earrings, and three rings. The rings were so pretty, and I loved nothing more than a big diamond. I had planned to give one of the bracelets to Lynda, but the rings were mine to keep.

After the lady left it was on! I walked over to Joe as soon as he closed the door. I pushed him against the door, and started taking his shirt off and kissing him. I felt his manhood growing with each kiss.

"Thank you for everything, Joe," I whispered in his ear while sucking on his neck. We started moving towards the bed slowly. He touched down on the bed first and I climbed on top of him. He flipped me over taking control. He kissed me so gently and unbuttoned my shirt and kissed on my breast. I moaned as I felt him remove my bra and take my breast into his mouth.

The feeling was unexplainable. Rico had never really made love to me. He was all about self. Joe caressed and sucked on my breast then moved down my body. He kissed my stomach, took my pants off with his mouth. He was so passionate that I could feel the wetness building. When he finally found my hidden treasure I was already in ecstasy. He was a pro at what he was doing. I tried to look down at him, but I got weak and my head fell right back down on the bed. His face was buried between my legs; this nigga was literally fucking me with his tongue.

"Damn Baby," I moaned as he pushed his head in harder. He then began nibbling on my clitoris while fingering me. I thought I was in heaven, about five minutes later I was ready for the real thing. His head was just a tease and I preferred penetration over oral sex any day.

"Come on," I reached for his head to bring him up closer to me. He tried to kiss me but I didn't play that, my juices or not.

I rolled him over and my body followed. I kissed on his chest and pulled his belt off. I put my hand in his pants, and pulled out his package. I wrapped my hand around it, and slowly went to work. I tried to remember everything Kiyah and Jade told me whenever we used to sit around and talk about sucking dick. I made sure my mouth was real wet, and I kept breathing. As I was moving up and down my tongue kept rotating around the tip of his penis. I continued rubbing it up and down while it was in my mouth.

"Fuck girl!" he yelled grabbing my hair. I guess that meant I was doing everything just right. I came up to grab the condom from off the night stand, and he came. "You the shit in every way," he said rolling over to his side of the bed.

"What the hell?" I was confused. Was it over? We hadn't even have sex yet and he was going to sleep like he had really put in work.

"What's wrong with you?" he asked pulling me towards him.

"Nothing," I said pissed off. I couldn't believe this nigga. I needed to get off too. I heard his breathing even out and I knew that signaled that my night was over.

Chapter Seventeen

The next morning I was awaken by the sound of a puppy barking. I woke up and there was an all black toy poodle jumping around the bed. He was black just like Joe. I sat up in the bed trying to catch the little cutie. “Whose dog is this Joe?”

“Baby, he yours,” he picked him up and handed him to me.

“Aww…he’s so cute,” I was holding him like he was a new born baby. “What should I name him?”

“I don’t know. He’s your dog…” Joe said getting off the bed.

“I’m going to call him BJ, for Baby Joe.” I kissed the dog’s nose and wondered what Lynda was going to say.

After having breakfast Joe and I got dressed and checked out. I was sad to be leaving. I’d had such a nice time besides getting dissed in the bed.

Joe was playing Dr. Dre “Fuck with Dre Day,” in the ride. I bobbed my head like I knew all the words.

“Oh here, I almost forgot,” Joe said reaching in the back seat. He handed me a Gucci bag that held a really nice Gucci purse.

"Baby, this is beautiful," I said kissing him even though I was still kind of mad at him about last night. He was doing some hell of making up.

"You can carry BJ or whatever you want to call him in it."

"In a Gucci bag?" I asked looking at him like he was crazy.

"Man stop tripping its more where that came from. You with me now. It's no price on nothing when it comes to you," he looked me in the eyes and I believed him.

Once I walked in the house Lynda went crazy. "Oh he is gorgeous!" She took him right out of my hands. "Where did you get him?"

She looked at me waiting for an answer. "I bought him from some lady. She only charged me $50." I jolted to my room to called Kiyah.

I was so relieved to finally have what I had prayed for for so badly; someone to take care of me. I thought Kiyah would be so glad to see I was playing my cards right; but she thought otherwise.

"Girl, are you fucking crazy?" she yelled before I could even really finish the story.

"No calm down, it's not even like that. He looks out for me. The relationship is just the icing on the cake." I said putting away all my things I had gotten from Joe. I was smiling so hard I knew she could feel it through the phone. Kiyah was just going to have to suck it up, because to me he was a keeper.

"Monnie, the grass may always look greener on the outside; but he is not what you think." She sounded as if I was truly disappointing her.

"I know Kiy… But I'm just in it for the money that's all," I explained as I caught BJ trying to go inside my closet. I caught him before he could start chewing on one of my shoes.

"That money and material stuff don't mean anything. Try getting back in school Monnie. Try having something that will have meaning in five years." She was really talking to me like I was her kid.

"I know but I'm just happy. I'm finally back like I was before my cousins left. My mama straight so I'm good. I'm going to go back to school just not right now. But call me later, I'm about to get dress. Love you," I was trying my best to rush her off the phone.

"Love you too, just think about this. All the clothes you are getting will be out of style next season. The guy, I pray that it's sooner than later, you'll realize is not for you. All the things you want you can get by going to school; but I'm not about to waste my breath. Good-bye." She hung up and the line went dead.

I knew she was mad and hurt, and I honestly knew it was very selfish of me but frankly I didn't give a fuck.

I made a call to the person that I couldn't get out of my mind. "Can I see you?" I asked when Dig picked up the phone.

"Yeah, meet me downtown in about ten minutes."

I was excited even though last time we were around each other things didn't go very well.

"Hey Ma, can I use your car for the day?" I knew she would say yes, she never really went anywhere.

"Yeah, put gas in there. I ran it out going back and forth to the mortgage company this morning."

"Why were you down there?" I asked thinking I knew we possibly couldn't be behind on bills. I stayed fronting her off with cash.

"I owe them two thousand by Thursday," she said like it was nothing. I could have slapped her. I didn't understand why she felt the need to keep these things from me.

"Why didn't you say something?" I looked at her waiting on her to answer, as if I was the mama.

"Why would I be telling you? You're my child. I take care of you. How are you going to get two thousand dollars anyway?"

She was walking towards me, and I knew this was not about to be pretty. "Mama, did you check your bible? You know sometimes you have money in there and be forgetting." I didn't get loud nor did I speak to her with an attitude.

"Yea, I had a thousand but I went to the casino with that," she said throwing her hands in the air as if it was nothing.

"You did what? You know what? I'm just about to get out of here," I kept my cool and stormed out the door. I wanted to choke the life out of her. Here I am thinking she's paying bills and she paying the casinos.

"Two thousand," I said out loud as I was making sure BJ was safe in the back seat. I knew I could get it. I had that hustle in me to do so. I also knew Joe would give it to me, but I didn't want him all in my personal business. She really has my blood boiling. I knew she had been to the casinos a few times over the past couple of weeks but not to lose money like that. With her not having a job, we damn sure didn't have it like that. Times like this I really missed Kyle and Ricardo, but they were gone and everything was on me now.

I hit Hart Plaza and decided to walk around with BJ. I was still so upset at Lynda. "If it's not one thing, it's another." I sat down on the bench by the water, and waited for Dig.

"Nice dog," he said walking up, grabbing my hand pulling me towards him.

"Thanks," I was smiling and he was smelling so good.

"How you doing?" he asked looking at me as if you noticed something different.

"Well I'm maintaining," I blushed, thinking of all the things I would do to this man.

"So how you been feeling, despite how everything is?"

It was something with Dig. I could always be truthful with him; and let it all out, and I did just that.

"Well honestly, I feel empty. I mean I have everything I was trying to gain back; but it's still something missing. I really miss my cousins." Soon as I said that I felt myself breath, like unwanted weight was just lifted off of me. I felt my emotions starting to rise, and hurriedly changed the subject.

"But let's not discuss me. How are you?" I said tapping his leg.

"I'm good. I had a long night. I know you did too at the Westin, huh?" he said raising his eyebrow.

"How you know where I was?" I said looking stupid. No matter what I did or what he heard; he never judged me. Our friendship remained the same, and I knew whenever I was done playing games he was going to be there to take me in with open arms.

"Come on Monnie, you know I be everywhere. So I see you got yourself a new boyfriend, and he's ten times worse than your old one," he was laughing at this point, and I was sitting there feeling like a big joke.

I never understood how everyone always knew my business. I only had three friends, well maybe two because I wasn't sure what was up with Jade. Half of the time they barely know what moves I make, so I didn't see how it would always get out.

"Naw, it's just business, but why you worried about me?"

"I really don't give a damn who you talk to long as you are safe, but this dude is nothing good. You should know that, but you hard headed and think you know everything so I'm going to let you find out the hard way. You need to at least get back in school though," he said standing up.

"Whatever…I'm going just not now." I stood following behind his actions.

"Don't no guy, well no smart guy want no dumb girl. He might not care about your future but trust me, it's important to have an education." He was looking down at me as we stood face to face.

"I'll be straight. I wish people would stop trying to tell me how to live my life." I started walking away. He was making me wish I hadn't come to meet up with him.

"Look, just be careful. Call me if you need me and you know that little money you making ain't going to last forever," he said walking behind me as I walked in front with BJ in my arms.

"Alright," I walked back to my mom's car, and he stood there watching making sure I got in safe and sound.

'Ugh… he really knew how to get under my skin,' I thought as I hopped back on the freeway. It was really starting to get to me. He was the only male outside my cousins who was bent on giving me a reality check.

When I got back to the house my mom said that Kristin had called. I started to call her back but she never had anything good to talk about so I passed. Instead, I called Joe, "Hey what's on the floor for tonight?" I asked looking in my closet, excited to wear something new.

"Well a little business mixed with pleasure so look good. Be there in an hour," he said. I could have sworn I heard a few female voices in the background and loud music. It sounded like he was already indulging in the pleasure part.

"Yep," I said then hung up. I pulled out an all black strapless dress, with some black stilettos to match. I knew Lynda was going to be up with a mouthful of questions for me, so I called Kiyah and put her up on game.

I was determined to return home with two thousand for the house, and maybe some extra for myself.

Chapter Eighteen

'I'm on a mission,' I thought as Joe pulled up. I got in and all eyes were on me.

"Damn, baby I said business, but you got me wanting all pleasure," he said rubbing my thigh.

"Oh really," I laughed. 'Just last night, you couldn't even hang with my ass,' I thought to myself.

Tonight I was feeling great, the dress was hugging me and I had a glow of happiness. Black was my color, it brought out the beauty of my caramel skin. I had worn my hair down and it hung to the center of my back.

"Where we going ?" I asked as he was speeding up Livernois.

"G's spot."

"Ain't that a strip club?" I asked. I'd never been inside a strip club and wasn't sure if I wanted to.

"Yeah, my boy owns it. I meet people here to do business from time to time," he said looking at me as if I should have already known. "I got a little something coming in tonight. Let's get this money first then we can party."

He touched my chin smiling. I had to admit I was starting to like him. A nigga who was about his business and always on the grind like I was is such a turn on.

He pulled right up to the valet and threw the big bouncer guy his keys. “I’ll keep it up front, Joe,” the guy called out as we got out.

“Cool,” Joe said grabbing a briefcase from the back seat. He put his arm around my waist and we walked into the club.

“Your booth is over there,” the bouncer said giving Joe some play as we walked through the door. I was amazed at the dancers, walking around with nothing on making the money. I would never have the courage to do that, but I’m not knocking them. Get it how you can; everybody has to eat.

“Come on we right here,” Joe said helping me into the booth. He started putting me on game about the deal tonight. “Now look, put this package in your purse. You going to meet my mans chick in the ladies room.”

He slid the package in my purse and once again I was in a situation I had never experienced but I told him I could handle it. I was so uncomfortable. A million scenarios ran through my head. What if she’s a cop or what if she tried to rob me? I was scared as ever, but I told him I could hold shit down.

“Look, they just walked in. When he gives me the signal I want you go to the bathroom,” he said pointing to the couple.

I looked over his shoulder and almost fell out the booth. The couple was Jade and Mack! I wanted to pass out. I hadn’t seen either of them since I busted them in Ricardo’s place. I had promised myself I was going to get them back, and they had the nerve to walk in here as if everything was good.

"Them?" I asked nervously.

"Your man here," Joe's friend said approaching our table to bring our drinks.

"Good looking," he grabbed our drinks and turned his attention back to me. "You alright? You look shook," he said immediately noticing my demeanor.

"Naw, baby. I'm straight. I'm ready to move when you say go," I said playing it off.

"You know how much we suppose to get right?" he said making sure I was up on game with everything.

"Yeah I got this," I reassured him.

"Alright, I let his ass slide a couple of times. If we got to cut our night short it's because my money short. Tonight he better not try that shit, or his night is going to be cut short. Go ahead Monnie," he said tapping me on my side.

"Alright I got you," I said downing my whole drink in one swallow. I had started putting my plan in effect as I walked over to the bathroom. I was laughing in my head at how devilish I could be. I was about to finally get my revenge. When I opened the bathroom door there this bitch was.

"Oh my God, Monnie! I miss you," she said wrapping her arms around me.

"I miss you too. When you start dating Mack?" I asked going along with this fake conversation like I really gave a fuck.

"Girl, just recently. I was going to tell ya'll but I was trying to see how he was going to act. He just had to get it," she said laughing.

"Ok, that's what's up," I said opening my purse.

"When you start messing with Joe? I heard he ain't nothing to play with."

"I keep hearing the same thing too, but he ain't nothing I can't handle. But enough of the small talk, let's do business," I said cutting her off. Something was telling me that she wasn't in on the shit but Mack still had to pay.

I reached down in my purse pulling out the package. She reached in hers and pulled out the money, then we exchanged.

"Okay call me girl. We gotta hang. I'll see you later," she said walking out of the bathroom.

I didn't even wait for the door to close before I made me way into the nearest stall.

"Oh, you will for sure," I said laughing at what I had planned. I started counting the money. I took two thousand and put it inside my panties. I put the other thirteen in my purse.

"Man, this is about to be so funny," I said out loud as I was opening the bathroom door.

I walked out scared as hell, but I wanted this to work so I had to keep it together. Joe was pretty smart, and if he knew I'd stolen from him he would kill me. I moved through the crowd trying to get back to the booth. A guy who I didn't know stopped me by grabbing my arm.

"Aye, Joe didn't introduce us. I'm Gee," he said holding onto my arm. "I saw you come in with him." He was so drunk he could barely pronounce his words.

"How are you?" I said trying my best to walk away. I knew Joe was looking and I didn't want no problems.

"Well I see you in a rush so if things don't work with you and Joe come through and holla at me shorty," he slurred as I walked off. "Damn, she got a body!" I heard him say as I faded into the crowd.

When I walked back to the booth, Joe was getting a dance and smoking a blunt.

"Party cut short," I whispered in his ear as I was sitting down.

"What? How much?" he yelled moving the stripper from in front of him.

"Two," I said sitting there with a smile on my face.

"So all you got was thirteen?" he said putting his blunt out.

"That's what I said, can you count," I lashed out like I was mad. I really didn't care what was going on.

"This nigga been handed too many lifelines, come on," he grabbed my arm making me spill half of my drink, and we headed out the door.

In the car Joe was making all kinds of phone calls. "Naw, he still in there. Do what you do best, man," I heard him say.

I was in my own world thinking of how good my plan had just worked out. I just killed two birds in one stone, my mama can pay the mortgage and I just got my revenge on Mack.

We pulled up to a red light, and I was looking out of the window thinking I really deserve a pat on the back. Joe must have felt different. I was so surprised when I felt the stinging sensation from the slap that he put across my face.

"What the fuck?" I yelled holding my left of my face.

"Bitch, I saw you over there flirting with Gee, and you tried to make me look dumb saying that slick shit. Can I count huh?" he was hollering at the top of his lungs and I was still sitting there in shock.

"Nigga, you got me fucked up!" I reached over trying to hit him back. By this time the light had changed and people were blowing their horns.

"Try me!" he yelled pushing me back into my seat. He sped off so people could not see us fight.

"Take me home," I screamed still holding my face.

"Naw, you going home with me," he hollered flying up the Lodge heading towards his house.

"I said I want to go home! I can't believe you just put your hands on me!" I said crying.

I was really wishing my cousins were home now. This dude wouldn't even be breathing. I didn't have anyone to call. I know Rico already wanted him and there was no way I was going to call him. He probably hated me now, Lynda was right. I cried as I realized I had no one. I guess I had Dig but his life was so perfect I didn't want him in the middle of my mess.

I wanted to just reach over and hurt him so bad, but I knew if I tried anything he would kill me.

"Shut up," his voice scared me to death. I sat there in complete silence which was what I had been told to do. The two men I needed and wanted were gone. My life wouldn't even be like this if they were here. The more I thought about it the more I cried. The bastard just turned the radio up on me, and didn't even think to say he was sorry or anything.

We pulled up in front of his place and I didn't make I move. I wanted to go home so bad. He walked around and opened my door.

"Monnie don't play with me. Get your ass out this car!" He snatched me up by my arm and pulled me out the car.

Once we got into the house he let my arm go and started talking trash, "Give me your purse. You probably didn't count the money right."

He took my purse out my hand, and I was so glad I put the two thousand in my panties.

"This nigga really tried to get me," he said after recounting the money. I got up to walk into the bathroom to see what he left my face looking like. "Where you going?" he turned and watched as I was walking off.

"To the bathroom and then to bed," I said all dry and raspy from crying. 'I swear he has to die for this. He is going to get what's coming to him,' I thought as I looked at my face in the mirror.

The whole left side of my face was bruised. My brown skin was now dark red. I washed my face off and walked into his room. I sat on the edge of his bed and thought about what had just happened.

For the first time in my life I was on my own, no help from my cousins or Lynda. I had my own hustle and I was getting money, but now I saw this shit comes with a price and I was not the girl to pay it. I had to come up with some way to get him. There was no way in hell I was letting this slide.

I got in the bed and prayed he stayed outside on the back porch. I peeked out the room and saw he was sitting on the couch smoking. I took the money out my panties and placed it in my purse. I had to get out of here. I put my shoes in my purse and ran to the front of the house. I opened the front door and was off into the wind. I ran so fast never looking back. I was scared as hell. I just knew I would hear his music coming behind me soon.

I dipped into a dark doorway of a nearby building and searched frantically for my cell. I called the one person who I knew would come get me.

"Dig!" I yelled once I heard his phone stop ringing.

"Yeah, what's wrong?" he said already knowing I was into something I should not have been in.

"I'm stranded! can you please come get me? I'm on Jefferson by the Ihop," I said looking around praying he would come and fast.

"Here I come! Don't move," he said then hung up.

I walked inside the Ihop and waited. I was lucky that he would even talk to me. I wasn't exactly doing what he expected of me. I had made up my mind. Dig was who I needed to be with. I was going to tell him I was ready as soon as he pulled up.

"About time," I said rushing out the door once I saw his car pulling into the parking lot.

"Hey," I said walking up to the car, not noticing there was a young lady sitting in the front passenger seat.

"Monnie, what happened?" he asked jumping out the car looking at my face and seeing I had no shoes on.

"I'm alright. Can you just take me to my friend's house?" I said cutting the conversation short. I had an attitude. How dare he bring a girl with him to get me?

"Monnie, this Ryan," he said as I hopped in the back.

"Hey," I said dryly not bothering to look her in the face. I was highly upset.

"Hey, how you doing?" she turned back looking at me, and putting her hand out.

"I'm fine," I said ignoring her hand.

My night had really turned into a nightmare. I had been slapped and to top it off Dig had totally disrespected me. I didn't know what to expect next. I couldn't wait until we pulled up at Kiyah's house.

"Call me if you need me," he said as I was opening the door. I didn't respond. I just closed the door. I prepared myself before I knocked on the door. I knew Kiyah was about to lose it when she saw my face.

Chapter Nineteen

"Oh my goodness! What happened to you, Monnie?" she said half way sleep reaching for my arm to pull me into the house.

"Joe hit me and I ran out of his house. Then I called Dig and he came to pick me up with a girl in the car," I was crying so hard, I could barely talk.

"Joe did what?" She woke completely up for that. I don't think she heard any other part of my story besides that.

"He-he hit me and I ran out his house…"

I fell into her arms. This was the one person I knew would always be here. I never doubted our friendship. I loved her like a real sister.

"Come on," she took me into her room, and calmed me down. "Why did he hit you?" She moved my hair from in front of my face. She rubbed my face and hugged me.

"Because he said I was trying to make a fool of him."

As much as I knew Kiyah wanted to say I told you so… she didn't.

"Everything is going to be alright. I don't want you dealing with him no more Monnie. Promise me that, I don't want you around him. You hear me?" She grabbed my face and I agreed.

I laid on her bed, and she ran me some bath water and gave me some clothes to put on. I slept at one end, and she was at the other. It reminded me of the days when we were younger and we would have sleepovers. The times I wished we could get back.

I had my eyes open looking at the ceiling thinking of one thing; my cousins. I missed them so much, and I didn't have the dignity to write or talk to them. It was like I was not ready to accept the whole concept of them leaving me.

I felt a tear roll down my face, I didn't wipe it. I let the tears continue to fall. I would rather cry every night before I would let them know how bad I needed and wanted them here with me.

Kiyah woke up before me, and I felt her moving getting out of the bed. I looked up and my head fell right back down to the pillow. I slept for about another hour.

"Wake up Monnie, you need to eat," I could hear her saying as I was opening my eyes.

"Aww…this for me Kiy," I grabbed my plate from her. Kiyah made the best pancakes ever.

"Girl shut up," she laughed handing me my juice when the door bell rung.

"Hold up," she said leaving the room.

I continued to eat until I heard Jade down stairs hollering and crying, "Kiyah, take me to the hospital please!"

She was hysterical, crying and screaming to Kiyah. I got up out the bed and walked slowly down the stairs.

"What happened?" I asked as I hit the bottom step.

"Mack got shot up last night! He in the hospital" Kiyah explained reaching for her keys.

"Wait I want to go too," I had the dumbest look on my face realizing my plan had actually worked. I hadn't thought about Jade's welfare at all. I was glad she was alright. In the car Jade continued to cry.

"It's going to be alright," I patted her on the back.

"But what if it's not? I love that boy," she faced me with tears rolling down her face.

Once we arrived to the hospital, Jade wasted no time. She went in the back to see him first, because he was in ICU and only could have two visitors at a time.

"Man, this is so messed up," I said sitting in the lobby with Kiyah.

"Yeah, but the lifestyle they live is an open invitation to either death or jail," Kiyah said watching the Tyra Show on the television that was mounted in the waiting room. Jade came out and Kiyah and I went into the back.

I was nervous as hell not knowing what to expect. Mack was connected to all kinds of cords and tubes. He looked like he was barely hanging onto life. I watched Kiyah's reaction and tried my best to fake it. In my opinion he should have died, because that's what could have happened to my cousin that he had set up.

Jade walked in and sat on the edge of his bed. She rubbed his hand and stared down at the man she had grown to love.

I didn't say a word afraid that my tone would speak the truth. Mack laid there so still I wondered if he was still with us. He was on life support and had a tube in his mouth and all kinds of IV's in his arm. His eyes were half way open and red, his face was cut all up.

"Who did this?" Kiyah asked touching Mack's arm.

"I don't know, but when we were leaving the club a black Cadillac was following us." When she said that I knew this was Joe's work.

I felt someone tap me on my shoulder as I was standing by the door, when I turned around no one was there.

"See what you've done," I heard a woman say into my ear, but when I turned around there was no one in sight.

"Did ya'll hear that?" I asked the girls trying not to be loud.

"Hear what?" Jade said looking up wiping her face.

"Nothing," I moved from the door, thinking I was tripping and started walking towards the bed.

"Your revenge has almost taken someone's life, you should feel bad," I heard the voice again and started waving my hands around me like it was a fly or something.

"I do…I do feel bad," I yelled out starting to cry.

"Monnie, what's wrong?" Kiyah grabbed me and asked. I raced out the room and ran into the ladies room.

"Leave me alone," I hollered yelling at the voice that was taunting me.

I looked at myself in the mirror and threw some water on my face, "Get it together Ar'Monnie," I said.

I did feel bad I had one of my best friends hurting because of my own selfish reasons. Now her boyfriend is in there lying on his death bed.

Mack was like family to me, but he had done the unthinkable when he betrayed my cousin. I felt like he needed to pay but not with his life. I was having conflicting feelings and I just needed to get out of there.

I walked out of the bathroom and the girls were standing right there, "Are you okay?" they asked.

"Yeah, I'm just ready to go," I said looking at Kiyah hoping she was too.

"Well thanks for the ride Kiyah. I love ya'll," Jade said sincerely.

"Love you too, but let's pray before we go," Kiyah said grabbing both our hands.

"Umm…I will meet you at the car," I said snatching my hand back. "Bye Jade, call me if you need me," I left straight out. "Pray?" I said out loud walking to the car. I didn't know who to pray to, or how.

Chapter Twenty

'Home Sweet Home,' I thought as I walked through the door. "Mama?" I called out. She didn't answer so I assumed she was gone. I went into the kitchen and sat down putting my head down on the table.

I was still tripping off the voice I had heard at the hospital. I knew what I heard, and I knew I wasn't going crazy. Lynda always told me to pray, and things would work themselves out. I just didn't want to be here to deal with any of this anymore.

I almost felt that death would be better than the way I was living. I was being abused mentally and physically. I was losing my purpose on earth. If this is what I had to look forward to then God take me! I don't want to be here, it's too much for me.

I walked upstairs and found boxes in the hallway leading into my room. "What the hell?" I said out loud walking in my room.

"About time you got here, help me," Lynda was packing up all my clothes.

"What are you doing? Where we going?" I asked looking confused.

"We're moving into a town house. I lost the house," said with no emotion. "We need a fresh start anyway."

"No you didn't. I have the money, Mama," I reached in my purse and pulled the money out and my mother's eyes lit up like Christmas.

"Where did you get this money from?" She snatched the money out of my hand. She stopped packing and ran downstairs and grabbed her purse.

"What are you doing?" I chased her down the stairs, and stopped when she fell at the bottom step.

"Monnie…help me I have a problem. I'm losing everything, you, this house and my mind."

She placed her head in my lap and cried. I didn't know exactly what it was she was talking about but I wanted nothing but for her to be happy. If giving her the money would make her happy then I was willing to give it all up.

"Mama, you can have it," I never looked down at her, I stared straight ahead. Tears rolled down my eyes, and hers rolled down my leg as she had her head lying on my leg. I needed to be close to her, she needed me more than ever.

I let my selfish thoughts of dying fade away once I knew I had a purpose and that was taking care of her.

She didn't take the money, instead she asked me to pay the rent up in our townhouse. The next day that is exactly what I did.

Chapter Twenty One

It had been six months since Joe had shown me his true colors. He called my phone ten times a day, but I had no words for him. I only talked with Kiyah, Jade sometimes and Kristin never called. I guess she was busy with school and all so I never attempted to call. Mack was in rehab, he had to learn to walk again and Jade was by his side every step of the way.

Ricardo and Kyle would always call on Sundays to talk with Lynda, but I never got on the phone. Lynda would go visit and write them, but I couldn't bring myself to go. I resigned to keeping them in my thoughts every day.

Rico had fallen off the radar. I never heard from him; and didn't plan to. Everyone said since Deon's death he hadn't been the same. The rumor was he determined to get Joe back. He wasn't going to let Deon die in vain.

Kiyah and I decided to go to the mall and I bumped into the guy Gee, from the strip club. I walked past him hoping that he wouldn't recognize me.

I knew my luck wasn't that good as I heard him say, "Aye, ain't that your girl?" I turned around and there Joe stood, tall and black.

"Come here Monnie," he said making his way towards me. I hadn't seen him since the night I ran out.

"Don't go over there," Kiyah said while we were standing in the middle of Northland.

"I'm not. I'm going to let him come over here," I stood with my hand on my hip wondering what could he possibly have to say to me?

"Hey man, I miss you. I went by your house, I see you don't live there anymore," he said trying to hug me.

"Yeah we moved," I said with an attitude.

"Oh, that's what's up. What you been up to?" he was smiling so hard, as if nothing had ever happened.

"Nothing. Just taking care of my mother and living. Anyway, it was nice seeing you but I have to go," I turned to walk away and he grabbed my arm.

"Monnie, I know I messed up, but just let me make it up to you. I mean it takes a real man to admit he was wrong, so don't act like we didn't have something good," He was talking as if he knew I was just going to forgive him right then and there. I shook my head and looked at Kiyah.

"We have to go," Kiyah tugged at my shirt and we were off.

"Monnie, the number still the same," he yelled as we were walking off.

"That boy is a fool if he thinks you about to mess back with him. He know he ain't shit." Kiyah went on and on, as we were getting in the car. I was in the passenger seat having thoughts of my own.

Joe did have the money flowing and I needed that right about now. Lynda's unemployment checks were just enough to take care of things but I missed that real money. I made it up in my mind that I would just deal with him a limited amount of time. Just enough to get that money again. It was like I was addicted to that lifestyle. I wasn't happy being average. I wasn't born to be average. Joe had the means to get me back to status.

Kiyah interrupted my thoughts, "Monnie, I know you not thinking about messing with him."

"Naw… I mean, I don't know," I said looking out the window.

"What do you mean you don't know? That boy slapped you. What other part of your body does he need to bruise to let you know he's not the one?"

I was used to her going on like this so I never got mad anymore.

"Don't mess with him, forget his money; make your own money. Whatever a guy gives you should be just extra's anyways."

"Kiyah…I hear you. Now just drop it." I was getting tired of her now.

We pulled up to her house and I could tell she was a little upset. "Kiy, I'm not going to mess with him I promise," I lied as we were getting out the car.

"Monnie, I'm serious," she said getting her bags from the car. I was mad because I hadn't been able to get what I wanted from the mall because our money was so tight. The idea of messing with Joe again was looking better and better.

"Hi ladies, Bye ladies," Tee, Kiyah's mom greeted us. As we were walking in, she was walking out. She stayed on the move, but made sure home was taken care of and Kiyah was fine with that.

I went upstairs to use the bathroom. I heard the door bell ring and Kiyah let someone in. I was surprised when I heard Kristin's voice. "I have to talk to you about something. Who is here with you?" Then they must have moved deeper into the house because I couldn't hear them anymore.

"Monnie, but she upstairs. Come in Kristin. What's wrong?"

She walked in and started talking. "Kiyah, I've been sleeping with Rico. I mean, we been talking for a while and I wanted to tell Monnie, but you know how she is," she whispered looking at the stairs.

I washed my hands and was walking out of the bathroom. As I hit the top of the stairs I could hear Kiyah talking, "Well you better tell her, before I do."

"Tell who, what?" I said walking down the stairs, looking at Kristin who I had not seen in ages.

"Look Monnie, I did something that I know was wrong. I'm telling you this because I really cherish our friendship," she sounded like she was about to cry, her voice was cracking.

"So what did you do?" I asked getting impatient.

"I…I slept with Rico," she said.

The old Monnie would have wanted to jump on her and beat her ass for this blatant violation of our friendship. But the new Monnie, that was about nothing but money and cared for no men except my cousins took over. "Well he is your headache now. He wasn't helping me with nothing," I brushed past her.

"Kiyah, call me later. Love you," I closed the door behind me. I pulled out my cell as I walked down the street and made a call.

"Joe, this Monnie come get me."

I would have been a fool, if I had not taken Joe up on his offer. I was going to let this man spoil me rotten, and take him for everything he had.

"What's up, baby? I knew you was going to forgive me," he said as I got in the car. "Here I picked this up for you," he said pulling out a diamond tennis bracelet. "I just wanted to show you how special you are."

I took the gift of apology from him and placed it on my wrist. It was beautiful. I figured I could get used to this.

Knowing Joe, this was just an example of what was yet to come.

“So I wasn’t special the night you hit me?” I said looking at him waiting to hear his response.

“Yeah you were. I was just having a bad night. I swear that will never happen again,” he said pulling off from in front of our complex. I worried about leaving Lynda home by herself, but I trusted her and it seemed like the therapy had been helping her.

“So, what we doing tonight?” I asked looking at Joe, hoping it was something exciting.

“We double dating tonight,” he said gauging my reaction. “We gon’ get something to eat at Starter’s.”

I was more anxious to see who it was we would be double dating with. I leaned back in my seat and enjoyed the ride. I flashed back to what Kristin had told me and honestly it did bother me. One because of the history I had with Rico but even more because she was supposed to be my friend. I shook those thoughts off and thought about what else I could get from Joe.

“We here,” Joe hit my leg, as we pulled up.

“Yes...let’s eat,” I said jumping out my seat.

We walked inside and waited to be seated. Once Joe and I were settled, another couple walked in looking as if they had just been in a fist fight.

"Aye man, what happened?" Joe asked standing and shaking hands with the guy.

"She don't know how to shut up, Bro," the guy said sitting down leaving her to stand and pull her seat out herself.

"This Mark, Monnie," Joe said pointing to him. I reached my hand out, and he kissed it.

"Nice to meet you," he said smiling.

"Hey. How you doing?" I said looking at Joe to assure him I wasn't making eye contact. I didn't want a repeat of what happened before.

"And how are you doing?" Joe said looking at the young lady that had walked in with Mark. She sat there with her glasses on covering her face and biting on her lip.

"I'm fine," she whispered, obviously holding back tears.

"That's my girl, Kat," Mark said barely even looking over to acknowledge her.

The waitress came over and took our orders and the guys made small talk while we waited. I tried to listen to every word while I faked like I was watching Sportscenter on one of the many televisions that were mounted around the bar. I didn't want to miss a beat, but my body was objecting.

"Hey I'll be back. I have to use the restroom," I said getting up from my seat. I saw Mark motion for his girl to go with me. I figured they wanted to take this opportunity to talk in private.

"Hey, I have to go too," she said pushing her chair back.

We walked into the ladies room and I rushed into a stall. I wasn't sure if she was talking to me or herself but she was ranting, "He thinks he is going to keep doing this to me, huh? He got another thing coming."

I came out and went to the sink to wash my hand. I looked into the mirror and she was on the right side of me staring at herself without her glasses on, or biting her lip. Her eye was swollen to the size of a golf ball and her lip looked as if she had been stung by a bee. I tried not to stare at her but it took me back to the night that Joe had slapped me around. She was being destroyed by a man, and knew she was but would not walk away.

"This is going to be you."

I turned around quickly looking scared, after hearing that same voice I had heard in the hospital.

"No it's not," I said looking around the restroom.

“What?” Kat said putting her glasses back on, looking at me.

“Oh, nothing,” I said throwing water on my face.

“Well I’m about to go back out here before his ass start tripping again.” Kat walked out leaving me alone.

‘Monnie, get it together. You’re just hearing things,’ I thought to myself. I wiped my face and opened the restroom door.

When I bent the corner I saw Mack standing at our table talking to Joe. I wanted to run back into the restroom, but Joe had already spotted me. I slowly walked back to the table dreading seeing Mack face to face.

“Monnie,” Mack said turning around as if he was shocked to see me with Joe.

“Hey Mack,” I said smiling slightly sitting back down next to Joe.

“Can I talk to you for a minute?”

I knew I would have been a fool to get up and talk to him in front of Joe, but Mack had been like family. He had almost lost his life, thanks to me.

“Sure,” I was so nervous, I almost tripped walking away from the table. I knew Joe was heated and I was scared to know what the consequences would be.

“Aye, man, what you doing with this guy? Your cousins would have a fit.” He placed his hand on my shoulder and continued to talk. “You don’t need to be around him, he got a lot of heat coming from people out here. You don’t need to be around him, he the one who got me shot,” he said pointing at one of his bullet wounds.

“That’s fucked up if he is the one that got you shot. I wish we knew who set my cousins up,” I said watching his face for a reaction. He wasn’t expecting that and his face told it all. “That’s fucked up ain’t it, fam? But don’t worry about me, I work with Joe, it’s nothing personal.” I could feel the heat radiating from Joe’s stare as I talked with Mack. I knew he was furious.

“Stay away from him! I’m not going to tell you again,” he said walking off as if he was one of my cousins. I guess his guilty conscience was getting the best of him.

I figured Jade must not have told him, I was the one who did the exchange with her that night in the bathroom. I wondered why. I put it together that Mack was the heat that was onto Joe, he was the one who wanted him.

“Yo, we about to get out of here,” Joe said leaving money on the table for the waitress.

“We didn’t even eat,” I said looking confused. Kat stood up and brushed past me as if she dropped something on the floor, and had to pick it up. We both stooped down to retrieve it.

"Get what you can, and get out. It's only going to get worse," she whispered.

"Let's go!" Joe said grabbing my arm. As we were walking out Mack was watching his every move. I saw him shake his head.

"You like making me mad, huh?" Joe said as we got into the car.

"Don't put your hands on me, Joe," I warned him. I was going to be ready this time, my hands were up and I wasn't going to let him get no shots at my face.

"Bitch, you don't tell me what to do! You going to embarrass me by talking to him?"

I knew this was coming and I didn't want the fight but I wasn't backing down.

"Joe, he is my cousin's man. I have to show him respect," I screamed.

"Fuck your cousin!"

From instinct alone, I slapped him and tried my best to punch him but he caught my fist.

"Bitch, are you crazy?" he said pulling over and I knew he was about to try and go to work. He threw my fist back down and grabbed my neck bashing my head into the dash board.

"You think you tough? Fuck you and your cousins! I will kill your ass and nobody would care," he screamed.

I lifted my head up and touched my nose. It was swollen and blood spilled out down on to my mouth.

"Please let me go!" I cried out as he still had his hand around my neck.

"Shut up!" he pushed my head back into the seat. I laid back in the seat. He pulled off and was making his way to one of his spots. For the whole ride I was quiet and thought of all the things he said to me, the one thing that stuck with me was "I will kill you and nobody would care."

"Get out!"

I jumped out as I was told to do. We walked in his spot and the guys were sitting around.

"What happened to her?" one of the guys asked, looking at me hold my nose with blood dripping down my arm.

"Nothing, she straight. Go clean yourself up." He pushed me towards the back and I walked back there feeling the lowest I had ever felt.

I could hear them all talking as I was walking into the back. I knew they felt sorry for me; but no one was sorrier than me.

I looked in the mirror and couldn't believe what was looking back at me.

Chapter Twenty Two

I cleaned myself up and opened the bathroom door. The door was cracked to the room across the hall. I crept out slowly and quiet. I closed the bathroom door, so the fellas would think I was still in there. When I opened the other door, there were bricks of cocaine everywhere! There was also a pile of money on a table. It looked like they were in the middle of counting it.

"What you doing in here?" A guy said walking behind me. I almost fainted, my body jumped with fear thinking it was Joe.

"Nothing I was…"

"You need to get on out of here. How you get caught up like this?" the guy asked me.

I had seen him somewhere before, I just couldn't put my finger on it.

"Gone ahead and take you a few stacks,' he said looking down the hall.

"Joe would kill me," I said touching my face.

"He won't know. I ain't no snitch," he said handing me a bag. I took the bag and was walking towards the money.

"Who are you anyways?" I said looking back at him grabbing money up. I would have been crazy to pass this opportunity up.

"My name is Cliff, and I work with Joe from time to time; but I ain't seen you and you ain't seen me," he said looking out the door making sure no one was coming.

"How am I going to get this bag out of here?" I stopped stuffing the bag and looked at him for help.

"Just leave it to me. Grab as much as you want and I will get it out to you."

I didn't know what this man was up to, but I didn't care. My greed took over and I wanted it all. "Alright," I said once I finished and gave the bag to him. I rushed back in the bathroom and closed the door and prayed that he wasn't going to give me up.

"Aye, hurry up! My mans about to drop you off," Joe yelled banging on the door.

"Okay," I said jumping at the sound of the banging. I opened the door and walked into the front to see who was dropping me off.

"He taking you home. Don't call me. I'll call you," Joe said not looking up at me standing over the table with his boys.

I laughed when he said it. I really didn't care. I was going to get the last laugh.

"So you ready?" Cliff said walking towards the door, holding it open for me. I wanted to just bust Joe in his head with something, but I knew his day was coming. In the car Cliff pulled two bags out and gave one to me.

I grabbed it smiling. I was so happy I couldn't wait to get home and see how much I had gotten away with.

"Why did you help me?" I said looking over at Cliff. I couldn't understand why he would risk everything for me. He was working for Joe not me.

"I don't know. Let's just say I owe someone a favor. I hate seeing good people hurt. He's always dogging women and I really didn't want to see you get hurt if he had caught you."

"Right here," I said before he passed my house up. "Thank you again," I said getting out the car.

"You're welcome. Keep your head up, it's going to be alright," he said smiling and rolling the window up. It was something about his smile that made me feel I knew him from somewhere but I couldn't put my finger on it.

I opened the house door, and Lynda was sitting on the couch drinking. "Mama, what are you doing?" I asked snatching the bottle out her hand. I should have just stayed home.

"Nothing, just having a drink. This is my first one," she said snatching the bottle back.

"Here, Kyle wrote you a letter. I told him you don't ever read his letters, but he said make sure you read this one."

She was holding the letter out and I wanted to throw it away like I did all the other ones but I couldn't.

"He sent you one too?" I asked looking at her thinking that must be why she was sitting here drinking.

"Yeah, he did," she said taking another swig. I shook my head and walked out.

I closed the door to my room. I was scared to read it; because I could only imagine what he had to say to me. People always told me the ones in jail knew things before people who wasn't in jail, so I knew the word was out about how I was living. I opened the letter and began to read,

"What's up Nay'onna... I'm just going to kick it straight to you. It's not what you do it's how you do it. I hope you out there being smart lil cuz. Karma is a bitch so be careful. I always told you what goes around definitely comes back around, and betrayal is the worst thing you can do to a loved one. Please just don't try and grow up too fast. Stay a kid long as you can. Remember to hold on to your loyalty and respect. You're a Wright, your heart don't pump no pussy blood! So remember, never let them see you sweat!

Here is something else to keep in mind; in this life you are not promised tomorrow. So take the bitter with the sweet and maintain. In these vicious streets, carry your heat and keep your mind on your money. Life's a gamble everybody got a number homie...Tale's of a Linwood Hustler. Kyle a.k.a Luciano

I Miss you and love you to death. You a li'l Rider but be smart..!! Pray for me Cuzo.

I wanted to break down, but I knew it would do nothing but make me angrier. Instead I was motivated. He was right, I needed to be smart. I wanted it all and I was going to get it.

That night I put all the money I had taken from Joe under my mattress. Lynda was getting it together but I wasn't trying to take any chances. I lied in my bed, and reflected back on my "guardian angel" of the night, Cliff. I knew I had seen him before but just didn't know where. My nose and head was killing me from Joe bashing my head so I knew I would be staying in tomorrow. I fell asleep thinking God only knows what's next for me.

Chapter Twenty Three

"Monnie, whose car is that out front?" Lynda said running into my room.

"What?" I said taking the cover from over my head still half sleep.

"Go look outside! There is a silver car out there with a bow on it!"

I opened the front door and Joe was out there leaning on the car.

"What are you doing here?" I said with an attitude.

"Man, come here" he demanded walking up the walkway. He pulled me out the door way and pointed to the car. It was a silver Grand Am, and the custom license plate read "4 U."

"I guess this is supposed to make everything okay again, huh?" I asked not even making eye contact with him. I was having an internal battle. I was happy to have my own car but I was still physically aching from the abuse from last night.

"No, but I'm sorry," he touched my face and ran his finger down my nose. The tender touch sent shots of fire through my whole head. My nose had to be broken but I didn't have the nerve to go to the doctor to get it checked out.

"Don't touch me," I pushed his hand off my face and noticed Lynda looking out the window. "I gotta go, I will call you later. Or let me guess, I can't call you. You'll call me," I said rolling my eyes at him.

"Yes, you can call me. I was just having a bad night; but I'm really sorry. I will never let this happen again. I just be under a lot of stress. Monnie, just take the car. I want you to have it." He threw me the keys. "Call me later, I'm sorry again," he said getting in his car.

"Who in the hell is that? That car is not staying here," Lynda said going off soon as I walked in the house.

"He is my friend and it's my car," I was locking the door trying to hurry back in my room.

"No it's not your car. It's not in your name. You don't even have your license," she followed me to my room, talking my ear off.

"Okay Ma, but I won't have to drive your car anymore," I said closing my door wishing she would shut up.

"You so hard headed. You think you know it all. Just watch what I tell you. Get your own, don't take that car," she warned me, still talking to me through the door.

I fell back onto my bed so happy to have my own car. I gripped the keys in my hand and thought of all the things I wanted to do today. I got up and looked in the mirror. My face was bruised; but I didn't care, he had gotten me a car. I wanted to leave Joe alone but I was addicted to the lifestyle that he could offer me.

I called my girl Kiyah and set up our day. It was time to shop! I was dressed and on my way to her in less than an hour. I absolutely loved my new car.

I put in my Jay-Z cd and was cruising to "Heart of the City." I pulled up in front of Kiyah's house and blew my horn. She came out looking like she had just seen a ghost. "Girl who car you done stole?" She got in looking around, waiting for my response.

I started to lie, but I couldn't, she was my best friend. "Joe bought it for me," I said pulling my glasses off my face. She was going to see it eventually so I rather get it out of the way now.

"Monnie! He hit you again?" She touched my face gently and her eyes welled up with tears.

"He was mad because I spoke to Mack, but he over it now and I have a car now," trying to make her see the bigger picture.

"No it's not over. He is going to keep doing this. A man only does what a woman allows him do to her. You need to leave him alone. Your body and life are priceless. Forget this car or any other gifts he has gotten for you!" She was pissed and I understood why, but I wanted her to know I had it all under control.

"Kiyah, I didn't come over here for no lecture, I came so you could roll with me today!" I was getting mad now. I know I was always letting her down but I just needed her to chill out for a minute.

"Well, I'm not rolling with you on this one. Call me when you come to your senses." She got out of the car and walked back into the house.

My feelings were so hurt when I saw her slam the door. I felt she like she taking things overboard but I knew it was only because she cared. I decided to be my own best friend. I wasn't going to let anyone steal my shine.

I pulled up to the mall and damn near ran to the doors. I was about to do what I did best, shop! I walked in and started spending. I saw things I knew Kiyah would love so I bought it for her anyways. I walked into Victoria Secrets and picked up two perfume sets for Lynda. I was just finishing up and was about to leave the mall when I saw Dig.

"What's up?" I said pushing him playfully as he ordered some cookies from Mrs. Fields.

"What up Monnie? I been calling you," he said ordering two orders.

"I know, I been busy. Dang! You gon' be big as a house if you eat all them cookies!"

"You know I ain't greedy! This ain't all for me," he said turning around and I could see Ryan walking towards him.

I hadn't seen her standing up that night they had come to pick me up. I noticed her stomach looked a little full.

"Hey you ready? I'm tired," she said grabbing the cookies from him.

"Yeah, you remember Monnie don't you?" he said looking back at me.

"Yeah, how are you? You haven't been getting into trouble or anything have you?" she said smiling, like I was a little kid or something.

"I'm fine, and yes trouble is staying out of my way," I said with a fake smile. "You seem to be putting on some weight." I knew that would get to her.

She had something for me though. "Yeah, we are having our first baby," she rubbed her stomach and looked at Dig.

I could have thrown up! Here I was always thinking when I was done running the streets and playing my games I was going to be with him.

"Oh, congratulations," I didn't wait for a response. I stormed off and Dig followed.

"I'll be right back," he said to Ryan running after me.

"Monnie wait!" he said grabbing my arm from behind.

"What?" I said snatching my arm turning to face him.

"What's your problem?" he asked as if he didn't know why I was pissed.

"What's my problem? You know how I felt about you and you just went out and got a girl. Now, you having a kid with her? How disrespectful is that? You acted like you cared about me." I was letting him have it. My face was beet red on top of the bruises. I was glad I still had my glasses on.

"What are you talking about? You never told me you felt any way about me. All that was ever on your mind was revenge and money! You never even said you liked me but I didn't care because I knew how I felt about you. I knew you had the potential to be the girl that I wanted but you shut me out! As far as disrespect, you the one who running around the city with a nigga who keep hitting you and buying you back. But I'm the one that's disrespectful, huh? You need to check yourself Monnie."

Those words smacked me in the face harder than the blows that Joe had hit me with. He continued his ranting.

"I loved you whether you were my girl or not. I'm always going to love and be here for you no matter what. You played around and now you mad because I'm not sitting around waiting on you. You need to really get your shit together you need to give yourself a reality check," he said pointing his finger in my face.

"Whatever Dig! Have a nice life," was all I could say as I held my head high and walked away.

Chapter Twenty Four

Kiyah walked into the police station with her mind made up. She refused to stand by and let her friend be destroyed by this man.

"How can we help you young lady?" The officer asked looking at Kiyah, he could tell she had been crying.

"My friend is dating an abusive drug dealer and he keeps mistreating her," she could barely get it out as her voice was cracking.

"Calm down," the officer walked from around the counter and handed her a Kleenex. He knew it was nothing he could really do, because her friend was the one that needed to be making the police report.

"I hate this man! He's dangerous and he has people do things to others. He pays them to do his dirty work, and he has her in the middle of everything," she looked up at the officer and he sat there quietly listening. He wanted to help her more than ever but he needed more than what she could give.

"How do you know he does all these things?" he said rubbing his chin.

"He stays in the streets and people know what he does. He's not smart at all and he uses her to be flashy and as his punching bag." She was getting angrier with every word she spoke.

"What's this young man's name?" he asked thinking it could only be one person.

"Joe," they spoke his name at the same time and Kiyah looked at him with a look of surprise on her face.

"You know him?"

"I don't know him personally, but a lot of people have it out for this guy. So don't worry, your friend will be okay. You're not the only one who is worried about her. Trust me when I say this, she has angels watching her," he smiled letting Kiyah know that everything was going to work itself out.

"I hope she does because I'm not trying to lose my best friend to his abuse." She was so sincere. Ar'monnie was her little sister, she was like blood and she wanted nothing but for her to be happy. But the happiness she was pursuing was nothing good

"You won't. I will take care of everything."

Kiyah smiled and suddenly felt better. It was something about his smile that was comforting.

"Now let me do my job, and stop worrying," he said standing up.

Kiyah got up and shook his hand, she was sure all of this was going to be over before she knew it. She thanked him again and walked outside to her car. When she turned on the radio, Eve's "*Love is blind*" was playing. She knew this was nothing but a sign. Her friend needed to get out or she was going to take him out!

***

I returned home with bags and a broken heart. I kept replaying the whole scenario over and over in my mind. Dig knew I was getting beat up and I was so embarrassed. He was moving on with his life while I settled for getting disrespected and beat up.

"How you doing?" The lady next door said as I was walking on my porch.

"Fine," I replied wondering why she is always sitting on the porch as I unlocked the door. No matter if it was hot, cold, raining or storming she was always outside. I never said much to her. Actually, this was the first time we ever exchanged words.

"Hey Ma, I got something for you." I handed the two bags to her and was walking away when she hit me with the big one.

"Rico called you. I want to ask you something and I want you to tell me the God honest truth."

I was still stuck on the statement that Rico had called.

"Yeah, Ma?" I leaned against her bedroom door thinking this was about to lead to nothing but some bull.

“Have I been a good mother to you?” she looked up at me as if I could really judge her. In my eyes she really couldn’t do any wrong. I loved her. Even on her worst days she was my favorite girl.

“Yes Ma, you are the best and always will be.” I walked into her room making my way on the bed with her. I never wanted her to question her character because I loved all of her.

“I don’t feel like it. I was so dependent on your cousins that when they left I couldn’t even help myself,” she said sadly.

Then the tears started to fall and I wasn’t ready for this. I kept my glasses on because not only didn’t I want her to see my tears but I didn’t want her to see the bruises that Joe left on my face.

“It’s okay, Ma. Everybody goes through something. We’re making it though. I told you I was going to take care of you and I am. I don’t want you to be stressing. I will make sure everything is like it was when they were out.” I wiped her face and she took my hand and placed it on top of hers.

“Will you go to therapy with me in two weeks?” My heart felt as if it had just stop beating. I wasn’t trying to go talk to someone who was going to be all in my head.

“Ma, I don’t know. I mean, I’m not with all that feelings and emotional stuff.” I stood up and was about to walk out.

"Sit down!"

This was the first time in a while that I'd heard Lynda sound like her old self. The one that didn't take no crap, or let me get away with half of the things I had been doing.

"Ma…" I strolled back over to the bed and sat with much attitude.

"You will go! Just like I'm confused and need someone to talk to, so do you." She grabbed my face and I knew she meant business. I remember as a child she would always do that whenever I was in deep trouble.

"Alright, it's a date," I said snatching my face back rubbing my cheeks. I walked out the room pissed. That was the last thing I ever planned to do, go to a therapist. I started putting away my clothes and that's when it dawned on me that she'd said Rico called. 'Maybe things were looking up,' I thought dialing his number.

Chapter Twenty Five

"What's up?" I said when he picked up. I didn't think he would ever dial my number again, especially since he slept with one of my best friends.

"Aye, we need to talk," he said like we were still together or something.

"About what?" I said as nonchalant as possible.

"Everything, man. I don't want there to be any bad blood between us. I would love to clear the air about some things," he explained.

"There's really nothing to talk about. We were done Rico, obviously before I even realized it. Far as bad blood you cool, I just lost so much respect for you after I heard you slept with Kristin." I didn't want him to know how hurt I was so I figured the less I said the better.

"See it's not what you think. Can I please come over?" he sounded like he was really trying to make peace so I agreed.

"Yeah come about twelve." I knew by then Lynda would be sleep and I could let him in the house. I really didn't care about him and Kristin but if he wanted to clear the air, I guess it wouldn't hurt.

He hit my phone at twelve on the nose to let me know he was outside. "When we were talking I couldn't pay you to be on time," I said trying to be funny when I opened the door.

"Yeah whatever," he walked into the living room and made himself comfortable.

"Well, have a seat why don't you?" I sat next to him and immediately smelled his cologne and noticed how good he looked. He was wearing all black and that was sending me over the edge. I looked away and got back to what the real reason he was here. "So what's up, let's talk," I folded my arms and sat back in the couch.

"Well you already know about me and Kristin, but I wanted to let you know myself. I'm digging her and she's digging me. I don't want no crap from you Monnie," he talked to me as if he knew I was a natural born trouble maker.

"Boy, I don't give two fucks about you and her. Be happy. You only messing with her to make me mad, but hey it's better her than me." I shrugged my shoulders and laughed. I knew Rico better than anybody and I knew damn well that boy wasn't in love with her.

"Ain't nobody thinking about you. This has nothing to do with you. I really like her, and I don't want you trying to mess with her or scare her." He turned to me, and I sat there still laughing. 'Yeah you like her, but you right back here with me.' I was singing SWV's, "*He's mine*" in my head as he continued to discuss her.

It also was a turn on that this boy took the time out of his night to come talk to me about his so called girl. It was like this was a set up for me to get him, and temptation was calling my name.

"Yeah alright, you only like her because she let you hit so fast." I crossed my legs which hiked my short nightie up even higher. My thigh was exposed and Rico was all eyes. He turned his head when he saw me watching him.

"Well, just let us be happy. She's worried about you I'm not. I know the games you play." He talked as if he was inviting me to break this sexual tension, and I was just about ready.

"Oh, you do?" I reached for his manhood, it was just as I expected. The boy was hard as a brick.

"Monnie, I really like Kristin," he said but still not moving my hand as I caressed his package.

"I do too, she's a nice girl," I said unzipping his pants. I was moving closer to him, and he wasn't pushing me away. He grabbed my ass and pulled me on top of him. He moved my panties to the side and helped position me so he could enter my body. I felt him completely as he pushed it all the way in, my body jumped right into motion with his and we were at each other's bodies like never before.

"Rico…" I moaned into his ear as I rode him. No matter how many guys I tried to like or tried to use to get over him, it never seemed to work. I was always so content with just him.

"Monnie, you feel so good," he moaned moving me up and down on him. I was feeling things I had never felt before between the two of us.

"I love you," I said as he flipped me over, and had my face in the couch. He had me positioned for doggy style and I was taking it.

"Monnie, throw it back," he demanded grabbing a hand full of my ass. I was moaning and screaming so loud, I put my head into the pillow so I wouldn't wake Lynda.

We went for another fifteen minutes before I heard him whisper, "I'm coming." He stroked me hard and long and fell on the side of me. I sat up and watched as some of his semen rolled back out of me, and that's when it hit me… we hadn't used a condom.

"Rico, didn't you put on a condom?" I jumped off the couch.

"No. You didn't say nothing. Any other time you tell me to put one on."

I could have slapped him, "I shouldn't have to tell you, you know that's a no-no. I'm not trying to have no kids, and I know you not." I pulled my night gown back down, and was ready for him to leave now. "Come on so I can walk you out."

'His ass don't give a damn about me or Kristin,' I thought to myself as I showed him out.

"Call me later," he said as I closed the door behind him not giving him a second thought.

I ran upstairs and jumped into the shower. I was praying that nothing bad would come out of this. My only concern was myself. I didn't care about him or his girl; because I knew damn well they didn't care about me.

I laughed at the fact that I had just fucked Kristin's supposed boyfriend. He would always come running back to me. I climbed in bed and turned my TV on, soon as I was getting comfortable the phone went to ringing.

"Hello?" I was pissed that someone would even call my house this late.

"We have an exchange tomorrow. So be ready about ten, Sweetie."

"Yeah Joe," I said before hanging up. I was going to go because this was money; but I was still going to get my revenge on him. The money I took from his house the other night wasn't enough, I wanted him to hurt. I rolled off my bed, and lifted the mattress to make sure all the money was still there. I had plans for the rest of the money.

I was still tripping on why Cliff would help me steal it. I wasn't going to worry my head about it. I had other plans. Joe's day was coming and I was going to be there to witness his downfall.

Chapter Twenty Six

I woke up and money was on my mind. I was ready and hoping to make some extra change for myself.

I was surprised but happy to see Kiyah's number on my phone. I thought she was still mad at me.

"Hey Kiyah," I said happily.

"Don't go with him!"

I thought this girl was losing her mind. "What are you talking about?" I knew exactly what she was talking about, but my mind was already made up.

"Don't go with Joe Monnie. Stay away from him." She was pleading again. I heard her, I just wasn't listening.

"Kiyah, I'm a big girl. I know what I'm doing. I will be fine, I promise. I gotta go though, love you and I'll call you later," I said before ending the conversation.

I was certain today was going to be a good day. Joe wasn't tripping and money was the motive today. Dressed in all black like always whenever I was with Joe. I walked outside and sat on the porch waiting on him to pull up.

I was surprised when I looked over and the old lady next door was sitting out this early with her portable TV.

"Good morning," she said softly when she noticed I was staring at her.

"Good morning," I turned my head wondering why she was always on the porch and by herself. I thought older people shouldn't be at home alone. I wanted to go over to talk to her but never got the courage to do so.

Joe hit the corner and I didn't blink twice, I flew to the car. As I was getting inside, I could see the older woman next door shaking her head as we were pulling off.

"So what's on the floor? What I gotta do?" I wanted to get straight to it, nothing but business from here on out.

"We going to meet this nigga. He supposed to be from out of town. He holding major work, so I'm meeting him at his people house. You are going to go in, and get the product. The money in the back, so just take this in with you." He grabbed the bag from the back and threw it on my lap.

Once again I was stuck in a situation where I was scared as shit. I wanted the money but I also wanted my future and life. I never knew what to expect whenever I was in something like this, I just hoped nothing went wrong.

Joe was flying on the freeway. We came up on Seven mile and Southfield. I looked around as we pulled up because I knew all this looked so familiar. He continued to drive and we passed Burt Road before we were pulling up to our destination.

"Go 'head. It's the house with the door open."

I sat there for a moment trying to think, where did I know this house from? I opened my door, and was feeling nothing but butterflies in my stomach. I put one leg out the car, and I felt nothing but fear come over my body. For the first time in my life I felt I was honestly doing something that was not right.

I got out and closed the car door. I took two deep breaths in and headed for the porch. I could hear a car behind me as I was walking. I turned around and it was Mack riding up the street. He slowed down and looked at me, once we made eye contact he sped off.

That was the moment I knew I was walking into nothing but trouble. “Hello,” I said knocking on the screen door. I knocked and rung the bell about three times. I looked back at the car at Joe, and waited for his signal to tell me to come back to the car.

Instead he gave me the signal to go in anyway. ‘What the hell?’ I thought as I opened the screen door. “Hello,” I said walking into the living room.

“Yeah, I will be right down,” the guy yelled from upstairs. I stood in the middle of the living room scared to sit or even breathe too loud.

“Joe sent you right?” the guy said running down the stairs. I recognized the voice and knew exactly whose house this was and the person we were dealing with. It was too late to run.

“Monnie?” Rico said coming down the stairs into the living room with a brief case in his hand.

"Rico," tears were already filling my eyes. I knew I had really fucked up this time.

"Man, what are you doing here and with Joe?" he asked confused.

"It's just business. I never wanted any of this. All I wanted was money and to take care of my family, but now he won't leave me alone." The tears started to fall and my mind was racing.

"So you're the girl that's been rolling with him, huh? So let me ask you this, were you the same girl in the house with him the day Deon got shot? Tell me the truth," his eyes were blood shot red. I saw there was no escape. I felt I should tell the truth because Joe didn't matter, he was going to get what was coming to him anyway. Rico was the love of my life and would always be.

"Yes, but…"

"But nothing, you knew and you shot at me. You ain't shit man!" He fell onto the couch and just looked at me with hatred in his eyes.

"Rico, I'm sorry this was all business. I never meant for nobody to get hurt, I swear. I don't want this lifestyle but I don't know how to get out!" I heard the car door closing and I glanced out the window. I saw Joe getting something out of his truck, I knew what was next. "Look we can finish this later? Just give me the stuff before he comes in here. He's crazy

Rico! He will kill me and you." I tugged on his arm hoping he would realize business still needed to be taken care of.

"Naw man, I'm about to kill him. This wasn't no exchange this was a set up. I'm gonna kill this nigga for Deon. I will deal with you later," he said pushing me off to the side and grabbed his gun from under the couch.

"Rico, please don't do this! He's crazy and I'm so sorry. Just listen to me, I never and I mean never thought all this was going to come just from me trying to make a dollar. I promise to change just please give me another chance," I begged him. As I saw Joe getting closer my heart was beating faster by the second.

"Bitch, get off me! You the reason my boy is dead and you tried to kill me. There is no second chance. You better hope I don't kill you after I kill him." He looked at me with nothing but hurt and pain in his eyes. I never in my life felt so low and dirty. I wanted my life to end at that very moment.

"What's taking you so long? I shouldn't have ever sent you in here. Take your dumb ass to the car," Joe said as he walked in the house. He snatched my arm and pushed me towards the door. I walked outside and I could hear Rico talking.

"So you killed my mans, huh?" he pointed his gun at Joe.

"What the fuck you talking about?" Joe stood there in complete shock.

"The nigga at your spot, that was my home boy and you killed him." Rico cocked his gun back and felt no sympathy. Joe followed his lead and lifted his gun up also.

"Man, Monnie pulled the trigger on him, not me," Joe lied. Rico had the drop on him and he was sweating bullets.

I ran to the car. After what I had just heard, I knew they both wanted to kill me. I jumped in the driver's seat and started the car up. I saw Mack's car and three other cars hit the corner. The three cars behind him were all undercover cop cars, Kyle put me up on game about them cars.

"What the hell?" I leaned back in my seat so no one could see me. Mack drove straight up the street, he never stopped. The three cars parked three houses down; but nobody got out. I looked in my rear view mirror and could see Mack parking his car.

I don't think he realized I was still in the car. I saw his every move. He opened his door and tucked his gun. He crept on the side of the house making his way in through the back.

I didn't know what to think next, it was like all my rotten plans were all blowing up in my face. I wasn't thinking about nothing else but what could be going on in that house. My eyes didn't leave off the front door.

I damn near jumped out my skin when someone knocked on the car window.

"Where's Joe?"

It was Cliff, the same guy who rescued me the other night. It was like he always came out of nowhere whenever I was in trouble.

“In the house, please go see what’s going on,” I said rolling down the window. I knew this was about to get ugly now that Joe’s boys were here. I was certain they were going to hurt Mack and Rico.

“Don’t worry I’m going to take care of everything. Just remember, never let them see you sweat,” Cliff said staring me straight in the eyes not even blinking. He nodded his head as if he was telling me to leave. He must have known what kind of affect those words had on me. Kyle would always tell me that if I was in a heated situation I couldn’t get myself out of, or if I was about to get myself into one.

“What?” I said thinking he must know Kyle but that would be impossible. He didn’t have to say it twice though, I wasn’t no fool. I started the car up and pulled off. I drove around the block and parked at the corner. I knew all too well what was about to happen. Suddenly shots rang out and interrupted the silence of the night. The hairs stood up on the back of my neck.

Chapter Twenty Seven

"Put the gun down" Mack said slowly walking into the living room pointing his gun at Joe.

"Man, what is you doing?" Joe said looking at Mack with his gun still pointed at Rico. The police were unloading the parked cars and surrounding the house.

"You tried to kill me. You thought I wasn't coming back for you?" Mack raised his eyebrows at Joe as if he was crazy to let that ride.

"Man, don't do this," Joe was scared as hell, with two guns pointed at him he didn't know what to do.

"Nigga, you fucked over too many people," Rico said. His finger was itching to pull the trigger.

"Man, I will kill both of ya'll niggas," Joe glanced at both Mack and Rico and thought what could be the odds. He let his mind believe he could kill both of them and walk out scott free.

"Dawg, fuck you!" Rico said letting his gun rip. He fired two shots missing Joe both times.

"Man…" Joe let his gun fire hitting Rico. Before he could aim at Mack, he was falling to the ground. "Shit" Joe said as he fell down, staring at Mack as he approached his body.

"I told you I would kill you." As he raised the gun to finish Joe, the cops were busting in.

"Get down and put your hands in the air!"

Mack dropped to his knees and placed the gun on the floor. Joe used every bit of strength in his body to keep breathing. No one ever looked over to see if Rico survived his shots.

Cliff walked in and over to Joe who immediately tried to sit up.

"Man, am I glad to see you. Get me out of here Dawg." Joe felt at ease now that one of his boys was there.

"Yeah I'm glad to see you too! You were one of my biggest busts. You are under arrest," Cliff pulled his badge out, and cuffed Joe.

"Man I can't go to jail! I've been shot," Joe said as he was being pulled up off the floor. "Don't worry after you get this wound touched up, you'll be heading downtown." Cliff picked him up and escorted him out.

"We got a dead one over here," A cop said checking Rico's pulse.

I sat at the corner and thought my eyes were deceiving me. "Cliff?" I squinted my eyes just to make sure I was seeing things clear. "How can this be?" I never thought to think he could be a cop. I saw him leading Mack and Joe out both in handcuffs. I waited to see them bring Rico out but that never happened.

"I got here as fast as I could! What happened?" Kristin pulled up behind me talking to one of the neighbors that stayed on the block.

"Well they were shooting in there, and I just called you." The lady said as Kristin began to cry. She didn't even speak to me when we finally noticed each other. I didn't expect her to.

"Oh my God!" Kristin ran to the house when she saw a stretcher come out with a white sheet over it. I followed and we both stopped right in front of the house as they rolled it by.

"Wait! Please wait!" I grabbed a hold to the bed, and wouldn't let it go. I had to see it for myself. Maybe there had been someone else in the house. I lifted the white sheet up and my world crashed in. It was my first love, my everything, the one who brought me more pain than happiness.

"No, No, No… get up please. I'm sorry! I'm so sorry!" I leaned on the stretcher and the medic tried to stop me. This couldn't be real.

"Move!" Kristin pushed me over, and touched Rico's head. She began to sob more and more. I stood there continuing to cry to myself. Cliff walked up and removed us from by him. They put him in the van and he was gone. I fell to my knees and cried. I couldn't believe this.

"This is not right! This is all my fault!" I pushed Cliff away as he tried to grab me.

"Come on! You need to get out of here now." He helped me up, but I just couldn't get the strength to get myself together.

"Bitch! You did this! All your lies and games. You're the reason Rico is dead, Joe is hurt and Mack is on his way to jail," Kristin said walking towards me, which lead the whole neighborhood to look at me.

"Kristin, I know you mad, but please don't walk up on me."

Cliff pushed me in the opposite direction. I strolled off to my car but was crying so bad I couldn't drive.

"I swear you are going to pay for this! You are going to get everything that is coming to you," Kristin screamed as I got into my car. She continued to yell and scream as I was pulling off.

"Monnie it's okay! You are going to be okay," I told myself as I was driving trying not to crash from crying. I kept wiping my face but the tears kept falling I was beyond hurt and guilty. I knew Kristin was right. This was all my fault.

This was all too much for me. I never thought my life would be like this. All I wanted was a normal life, to be a regular teenager. I needed my cousins. I needed the love and attention I got when they were out. I needed Rico back and not as a mate, but as my friend. I wanted the girls and me to be able to sit around and laugh again. I wanted all the love back, and I never knew how much I needed it until now.

My luck had run out and I was down with no one to run to. I pulled over on the freeway and looked out my car window at the sky. You couldn't tell me there was a God. So much bad stuff had happened to me, if there really was one he would have come to help me.

I sat there and cried for about ten minutes before I was able to drive home. All I could think of was Rico. I never imagined my life without him. I had lost my cousins and now him. It was worse because I was losing him to death. I pulled up in front of my house, and my body was still shaking. I took a deep breath, and thought of what I could tell Lynda.

The news spread like wildfire in the hood. I knew Lynda would be asking me about it soon. Rico was her favorite out of all the male friends I had, and she also respected him as my boy friend. She was going to definitely be questioning the situation. I stepped out the car, and my body felt numb like I was walking in someone else's shoes; or living someone else's life!

Chapter Twenty Eight

I must admit I wanted revenge on Rico but nothing close to death. I put my game face on and opened my car door. I noticed Lynda's car was gone.

"Hey Miss Alice, did you see my mother leave?" I walked over to her porch and asked. It was like this lady saw right through me.

"She heard about some shooting and went looking for you," she said watering her plants not even looking in my direction.

"Oh my God," I covered my mouth panicking. She was really going to be questioning me when she got back.

"She should be back shortly. I take it things didn't go as planned, huh?"

I looked at her as if she was crossing all the wrong lines. How did she seem to know something popped off?

"Excuse me?" I was holding on to the last bit of strength I had in me. I was about to break down.

"Life is what you make it, believe in me." She turned around and faced me. Her voice reminded me of the voice I had been hearing in my head from time to time.

"I don't know what you're talking about." I started to walk off but she kept talking.

"Just don't let your heart overpower your mind, Ar'Monnie. Be smart."

She had sat on the bottom step of the porch, and I turned around and joined her. I was drawn to her voice. Even if I didn't want to listen, my body was moving on its own. I never listened to anything anybody had to say. "It's too late for me," I sobbed. "I believe this is all life has to offer me. I'm done."

I hated shedding tears in front of someone. It was a sign of weakness and I had been trying so hard to show that I wasn't weak, but at this point in my life I didn't care. I had lost half of me when my cousins left and today I had lost what was left. These past months had been like hell and I truly believed things couldn't get any worse.

"Never say you're done. Don't you know the devil can hear that? You're making it easier for him to take over. You are a fighter and a child of God, so you are never done."

I believed every word she said, and I had never even taken the time to get to know my God. "I feel like God has forgotten about me. I mean, why does he keep letting all this stuff happen to me?" It was so hard to hear about all the good things he does, but it was never for me.

"That's all a part of his plan. He has already set things up for you. You have to meet him half-way. You have to want to help yourself first before someone else can help you." She placed her hand gently on my knee, and I looked up at her. She made me believe. I had never felt so strong in my life until she spoke those words to me.

"You think he will forgive me? I think I've done too much to try and turn around now." That was my biggest fear of change, not knowing if I could handle it or what it had in store for me.

"Of course, but you have to be willing to forgive yourself first, Monnie. See, life will throw all kind of curve balls at you. You have to be ready to dodge them and keep your focus. If you see it, you can have it. If you think it, you can do it. Just believe in you." She reached her arms out and I leaned in. I didn't have to let it all out in words it was like she read me and knew everything.

"It's so hard," I said as I sobbed on her shoulder. I peeked over and could see Lynda pulling up into the parking lot. "There's my Mama," I jumped up and wiped my face. I don't think I had ever been this happy in my life to see her.

"Oh my God! Monnie, are you okay? Rico got killed baby." She grabbed me close to her chest. I felt safe again and loved. I haven't felt this way since Ricardo and Kyle.

"Yes, I'm okay," she looked at my face to see if I was lying, but this time I was telling the truth. I was okay. I just needed to face all my pain and learn how to channel it into something worth having.

"Come on in the house." She put her arm around me and we headed in.

"Go head Ma. I will be right in." I ran over to Miss Alice and hugged her again. "Thank you so much. I never let anyone see me at my worst or when I'm weak."

"Don't thank me and you're not at your worst. Your weakest and worse moments are your best and strongest moments because it teaches you how to survive." She stood up and hugged me again.

"You're right. Thank you, again," I said walking off. I thought I could get use to this. I felt so much love coming from her, and I really appreciated it.

"Mama," I called her name walking into the house.

"In here."

I joined her in the kitchen as she was starting dinner. "Mama, you cooking?" I was so surprised she hadn't cooked since we lived on Oakman, back when things were straight.

"Yes, are you sure you okay?" she kept checking my facial expressions for any signs of me being down or depressed. I was but I knew that things would work out. I did feel guilty but I was going to deal with this pain my way. I wanted out.

"Yeah, I'm good," I said as the phone began to ring. I raced over to the counter and it was Dig. I took a deep breath before I answered. I knew our last exchange had been bad and I didn't want him to think I was still tripping.

"Are you okay? I heard about your boyfriend. I'm really sorry, Monnie," he said sympathetically. There weren't any traces of bitterness in his voice and that further showed me that he was down for me and he wasn't going anywhere.

"I'm ok. Thanks for calling," I said trying to keep my emotions in check.

"Do you need to talk?" he asked, and before I could answer he was answering for me. "I will just come get you in about an hour."

"Naw, I just want to be home. I think I should be by myself for awhile." I would have loved to be around him, but I needed to spend time with myself, to get to know me. I wanted the change I had avoided all this time. I wanted to depend on myself for a change.

"Will I definitely understand that, but you know the streets are talking. So just please be careful out here. Niggas think you set all of them up."

"Well I didn't. I was just in the wrong place at the wrong time." I snapped on him and didn't mean too, but it was like I couldn't win for losing. Here I was wanting to change, wanting to get out the game and it was still running towards me. "Look I have to go," I said once I saw Lynda looking at me.

"Okay, just promise you will call me if you need me."

"Promise," I said hanging up.

Deep down I wanted revenge on Joe for shooting Rico, but something told me he was going to get dealt with either way.

"Who was that?" Lynda asked as I was hanging the phone on the charger.

"My friend, nobody really." I was hoping she was willing to drop the conversation.

"Well, I still want you to go to therapy with me, and after what happened today I really think you should go."

At first I was truly opposed to going, but I could the change in her; so I wondered what they could offer me.

I said, "I'll go, Ma."

We ate dinner together and I made sure that she was confident that I was ok. She kept looking to see if I was near a breakdown but I held it in until I got to my room. I let it out all into my pillow. I cried for change, for my cousins and for Rico. What hurt me the most was feeling that Rico had died mad at me. I loved him and I never meant to have his death sitting on my heart. His or Deon's. I wondered was my life worth trying to get back. Once again I hit rock bottom and didn't know how I was going to get back up!

Chapter Twenty Nine

I was shocked from my thoughts by the sound of my mother screaming my name. I rushed into the room to find her standing at the window looking outside at what appeared to be flames. I ran to the window and couldn't believe my eyes!

Someone had fire bombed Lynda's car! The car was engulfed in flames but I noticed a note taped to the back of the driver's seat. I could already hear the sirens from the fire trucks as I ran outside and jumped off the porch, with my mother on my heels. The note had burned by the time I got out there and I couldn't have gotten to it anyway.

"Lynda, are ya'll okay?" Miss Alice asked coming out on her porch with the rest of the neighbors. I was furious as I stood there watching my mother's car go up in flames. It took them all of thirty minutes to put the fire out and it was totaled.

The fireman was talking with Lynda and going over what she needed to do. I watched them load the car onto the flatbed. I could feel the anger rising as I started going towards the house.

"Don't fall into it," Miss. Alice said walking past me going back into her house. She was right and I wasn't going to fall into it. I didn't even know who had done this.

Kiyah was ringing my phone when I got back in the house. "Monnie… I'm so sorry I couldn't call you yesterday, so much was going on. Are you okay, do you need me to come over?" Kiyah was talking twenty words per second.

"Yes, can you come over? I really need you and I don't want to leave my mom home by herself," I said looking out the window. She was still outside talking to the neighbors.

"I'll be over shortly," she said hanging up.

I could always count on her no matter what the situation was between me and her; her love for me never changed.

I walked to my room, and didn't know where to start. I wanted out but something just kept calling me in. It was like Miss. Alice said the devil had heard me now he was working his plan on me. I thought of writing my cousins to ask them where to go from here. I wanted to ask them what would they do if they were in my shoes. It was times like this that I really needed them. I knew if they were around, I wouldn't be going through any of this.

I sat on my floor and pulled out my memory box from under my bed. "Wow," I said as I picked up a picture of me and the girls. It was crazy how we had grown apart. Kiyah and I were the only ones that were still close.

I skimmed through some more pictures, and came across me and Rico. "I swear I never meant to hurt you, and if I could do just one thing to prove to you how sorry I am, I would." I kissed the picture as I began to cry. I thought of all the memories we had together.

"I love you," I said kissing the picture again, before I put the box back under my bed.

"Come here," Kiyah said walking into my room.

"I'm fine," I said giving her a hug.

"I love you Monnie, but I told you not to go." She couldn't wait to lecture me.

"Kiyah, not today please. It wasn't even what you think. It was a set up from the beginning. I was just at the wrong place at the wrong time." I kept telling people that, and actually started believing it myself. I could have avoided all of this if I would have just stayed home, but I was chasing that money.

"Well I'm here for you. Kristin has been taking it pretty hard too. Jade's pretty messed up because Mack is getting charged with murdering Rico."

"But he didn't shoot him, Joe did." Even though I wasn't in the house, I knew it was Joe.

"Well like you said, Mack just was in the wrong place at the wrong time too. I heard you were on the block after it happened. I didn't know you were there when it actually went down."

"I wasn't there. I got there after the shooting. People were calling me telling me what happened, but I know Joe did it." I was happy Cliff had told me to leave from over there. Joe was sending out the message that I was a rat and I prayed no one believed him.

"I'm just happy you're safe. I know I never cared for Rico but I would never wish death upon anyone," she said sitting on my bed.

"I know. I just wish I could do something to make him happy. Something to make me know he is at peace with me," I said thinking I wanted nothing more but for him to forgive me.

"Go back to school, graduate. That's something he is not going to be able to do. You will be eighteen next month, you missed a lot of the 12th grade but it's not too late."

For once in my life I agreed with Kiyah, but I was embarrassed about going back. "Ya'll got 12th grade credits, I don't. I'm not going to graduate on time," I said looking at her like she was the dumb one for saying that to me.

"Okay and whose fault is that? It's yours Monnie, but it's not too late. What's this?" she asked picking up my grandmother's journal off the floor. I must have forgotten to but it back in my memory box.

"Nothing, give me that." I snatched it out of her hand. I didn't want her to read anything in there.

"Dang!" she said sitting back on the bed. We sat in my room and talked for about three hours. Kiyah had convinced me that school should be the next step for me and I was ready for that.

Reality

"Come on I need you to take me home, I got dropped off," Kiyah said grabbing her things heading to the door.

"Let me check on my mom then we can go." I peeked in her room, and she was knocked out. She had an interview in the morning and we were going to therapy so she needed to get some sleep.

I dropped Kiyah off and was headed home when I noticed a police cruiser in my rear view mirror. Thankfully I had my seat belt on. I made sure I was doing the exact speed limit. They tailed me for another block or two then they turned on their lights. I wasn't doing anything wrong, so I didn't know what they wanted. I pulled over to the side and turned my car off.

"Yes officer?" I said rolling my window down.

"License and registration, ma'am," he said with the flash light all in my face and inside the car.

"I left my purse at home, so I don't have them on me."

I knew he was on some bullshit when he continued to nag me. "I'm going to need you to step out of the car."

I opened my door, and wanted to literally take off running; not from the cop but from everything. The pain and drama seemed as if it was not going to let up.

The other cop that had remained in the car got out and walked up to the car. What he said next I could not believe!

"Carson, this vehicle has been reported stolen," he said to his partner.

"No it's not! My friend got me this car," I protested. The cop told me to be quiet. I was getting scared as shit. I was not about to go down for this.

"You are going to have to come downtown with us. We need you to answer a couple of questions," he said already cuffing me.

"No, this is a mistake…" I cried out as I was being pushed into the back seat of the police car. I cried all the way to the station.

"Let's go," Carson said opening the door grabbing my arm. He took me in through some back way, and I didn't know what to expect. I made sure I stopped crying before anyone else saw me.

"We have a new one," Carson partner said, taking the cuffs off of me. They took me into this cold dark room with nothing but a table and a chair in there.

"Is this the holding area? Don't I get a phone call or something?" I asked looking around.

"No, just go sit down."

I walked into the room and sat down. I promised myself when I got out of there that I would never go back. I laid my head on the cold table, and started to think.

Reality

I wanted to let go. Let go of everything, all the hurt and pain. I needed to start fresh with nothing but happiness and joy. I never pictured my life taking this many detours. I wasn't going to give up though.

"Why me?" I said aloud in the dark room.

"I wonder the same thing too, why you?" Cliff said walking into the room with a folder in his hand.

"What are you doing in here?" I asked looking up at him.

"I work here, and this here is your file. It's my personal one on you," he smiled opening the folder up.

I flipped through the pictures and I wasn't a bit surprised. They had pictures of me from the day they had come to get Ricardo up to the day of the shooting.

"Look this is between you and I. Nobody knows I have been looking out for you," Cliff said pulling up a chair sitting across from me.

"Why though, why would you or anybody take the time to help me?" I seriously wanted to know, the guilt of all I had done made me feel worthless.

"You may not think it, or feel it but it is at least one person in this world that loves you to death. When your cousins were out here I tried to get in their circle but they wouldn't let me penetrate, so I had to go with Joe. I watched them from afar and I have much respect for them. They just got caught up in a set up and I still can't knock what they did. But I'm on the good guy's team so I have to do my job. But I know how much they love you and I decided that I would look out. Ar'Monnie, you just need to grow up, and trust me it was not easy keeping up with you making sure you didn't get into anything too deep," He said placing his hand on his forehead.

"What's that supposed to mean?" I said laughing already knowing I was nothing but a mess.

"You know exactly what I mean. But, Joe reported your car stolen. We have to take it because it's in his name. You can call a ride and get out of here and I will take care of everything else."

"Okay, ya'll can have the car. I shouldn't have ever accepted it in the first place."

Cliff handed me his cell phone but realized that I didn't have anyone to call. It was late and I know Lynda was knocked out. "Damn, I need a ride," I thought out loud. I started to call Dig but thought twice. He had his own life and other things to worry about now. So I decided to call on my backbone, "Kiyah please come get me, I'm at the 12th precinct. I will tell you everything when you get here."

That was all I had to say and my girl was on her way. Twenty minutes passed and I was starting to get antsy, "Where is she?" I folded my arms thinking I could really use a wish right about now.

I jumped up once I heard them call my name. I waited for the man to let me out. I rushed out to thank Kiyah for coming to get me but was surprised to see Dig standing there.

"What are you doing here?" I said frowning.

"Well a thank you would have been nice," he said as we were walking out the door. I saw Kiyah sitting in the car.

"What happened?" she got out hugging me.

"Why you didn't come by yourself, and how did you get in touch with Dig?"

"You needed someone 18 or older to get you out, so I called him. I always have a number for any guy you talk to. Just in case something happens, because from the looks of things you don't have very good judgment," she said rolling her eyes upwards.

Her comment lightened the mood. I jumped in the car with them and thanked Dig the way I should have when I first saw him.

"Thank you again" I said as I was getting out the car. I had stayed in the back seat after we dropped Kiyah off because I still felt bad for acting so crazy at the mall.

"You're welcome. I told you to just call me if you need me. I got you." He smiled and I knew then he really wasn't going to leave my side. He was truly a good person at heart, and I wasn't going to let our friendship end because of my pride. I strolled into the house, and checked on Lynda. She was still sleeping and I knew the coast was clear.

"June 1st," I said out loud as I walked into my room. "What a day."

I sat down and tried to piece some things together. It had to be Joe that burned my mama's car. The notes were from him. I know he felt that I had crossed him. Betrayal on the street meant he wanted me dead. I was going to get him back, but this time not with violence but with words. I always had a slick mouth and I was going to use it to my advantage.

"Just one more thing before I hang the game up," I thought as I fell back in my bed.

Chapter Thirty

"Let's go! We're going to be late," Lynda was snatching the covers off of me.

"Late for what?" I said sitting up in my bed.

"Therapy…now come on," she yelled walking out my room. I was dressed in less than thirty minutes.

On the way there I started to think of Rico. His funeral was tomorrow and I didn't know if I was ready for that or not. To see him lying there and to know this was all because of me. My eyes got watery just thinking about it.

"Hurry up, we're late" Lynda said jumping out the car. I walked behind her. I wasn't too excited about this but a promise was a promise, and I didn't want to let her down. I could see the change in her. She was happy again and that made me happy. I knew she wouldn't stay down long. She always told me a strong woman never stays down too long.

"Hello Ms. Gray," Lynda walked into the office and I followed.

"Hi Lynda and you must be the famous Ar'monnie?" she said reaching her hand out for mine.

"Yes, how are you," I said fake smiling sitting down on her couch.

"Well let's get to it. What's new?" she said taking out a note pad and pen.

"Well," Lynda started, "I finally got a job!"

I was happy for her but wondered why she hadn't told me. "Ma, why didn't you tell me this morning when you got back?" I folded my arms waiting on her answer.

"I wanted to wait until we got here. Are you happy?"

"Of course, I am." I knew that made her feel good, to have her independence back.

"So what else is going on?" Ms. Gray turned and faced me like she was ready to get inside my head.

"Nothing," I said once I noticed both of them were facing me.

"So how have you been feeling since the death of your boyfriend?" she just cut straight to it.

"I'm fine," I said angry knowing Lynda couldn't hold water.

"Monnie… I brought you here so you could deal with your feelings. I know you are hurting, and I want you to know everything is going to be alright. Do you want me to leave out the room? Will you feel more comfortable then?"

Lynda was trying her best to break me, but I wasn't having it. "No, I don't think it would make a difference," I said rolling my eyes.

"Yes Lynda. I do think you should step out and let us talk," Ms. Gray said getting up to open the door for her.

"Okay, I will be right outside the door Monnie."

As she walked out, I knew this was definitely about to be one of the worst hours of my life.

"Look, this will only be harder if you keep trying to play this role," she said closing the door after my Mom.

"I'm not playing any roles. I told you, I'm cool," I said readjusting my body on the couch.

"Ar'Monnie, your body language is telling on you. You can't even sit still. Moving around won't help you shake these problems," she said smiling. Nothing I said seemed to ruffle her feathers.

"So what do you want to talk about?" I said shaking my head, irritated already.

"You and what's behind that mask of yours. Who is the real Ar'monnie Wright?"

"I'm a girl who loves my family just like anyone else. I will do whatever it takes to protect and feed them. There you have it," I said moving my head from side to side.

"So at what cost will it take for you to see that this is not some fairy tale. Because I'm pretty sure things get rough out there for you." She placed her fingers on her chin, and looked at me like she knew the ropes to the life I was living.

"It pays to be the boss, and sometimes you have to play the cards you are dealt. That's what I do, well I did. If a situation came up that might turn out bad, I made the decision that would bring me the money. Money and revenge keeps me happy. Knowing that someone got over on me makes me so angry. Someone trying to hurt me or my family has to pay," I said feeling the anger brimming again. I didn't blink twice when I told her that. I wanted her to know that I meant that from the bottom of my heart.

"Why do you feel you have to always get somebody, or hurt people?" She asked sitting on the edge of her seat waiting to hear my answer.

"That's how life is. I live by this motto: One who does wrong MUST NOT GO UNPUNISHED." I crossed my legs and started to shake my foot. I was ready to go and I was feeling like myself again. Money and revenge! The bitch is back. I sang out loud in my head while she was writing on her pad; I didn't even care what she was writing.

"Who hurt you? Or should I say what hurt you?" She knew this would trigger me. This was going to unleash all of the wounds that never really healed.

"My…My cousins, and Rico and myself." I had never admitted any of that. I buried all that in the back of my head and the pain in the back of my heart.

"Are you done?" Lynda busted in right in time.

"Yes, we are." I hopped up and walked out the door. I grabbed Lynda's arm and we were out of there.

"See you again next week, Ar'monnie," Ms. Gray yelled as we were walking down the hallway. I was already out the door not giving it a second thought.

"Do you feel better?" Lynda asked driving up 96.

"No, I feel worse." I knew what I had said was the reason to all my actions. I was bitter and hurt, and didn't know which way to turn. For the rest of the ride, I laid my head back and thought about what Miss. Alice had told me, was she right? Could I start completely over, could I get my life back on track?

"Home sweet home," Lynda said tapping me thinking I was asleep.

"Finally."

Miss. Alice was sitting on the porch reading.

"Hey how are you today?" I said sitting next to her.

"Fine and you?" she smiled. Her smile always gave me the feeling of love and peace.

"I'm okay. You read the bible every day?" I asked looking to see what she was reading.

"Yes, and I have something I want you to read." She flipped through some pages and stopped at Psalms 27. "Here read this," she placed it in my lap and I wanted to give her the book back. I had never even read one passage from the bible. I didn't think I would ever understand it totally.

"I don't…." I moved my hands trying my best to explain to her, that it was nothing against her; but I just felt I wasn't ready for this.

"You can, you want forgiveness and to start over, right? So read. Understand that there is a plan for you."

I began to read and the words were like music to my ears. I was in tune with the scripture and could feel my heart settling.

The one part that stuck out to me was, "*When your father and mother forsake you, then the Lord will take care of you.*" I closed the book and asked her could I take it home.

"Yes, it's all yours," she patted me on the back and I went home. I wondered if my grandmother had still been alive would she have been just like Miss. Alice? To me Miss. Alice was like my fairy godmother and I was accepting all the help she was trying to offer me.

I went into my room and read the same part again. It was absolutely true, no matter who leaves me; the Lord will never forsake me. That's the moment I accepted all the change in my life. I knew then that someone in this world loved me. There was someone in this world that was not ever going to give up on me. All this time I had been searching for love and it was right in front of me. GOD gives unconditional love to all of his children and I was one of them.

No, my father really wasn't around. No, my cousins weren't around anymore. Rico's death had brought me nothing but sorrow; but someone still loved me through out of all my faults and it was God. I started to believe and wanted closure to everything. I was going to take everything one step at a time. I knew exactly what was going to be my next move!

Chapter Thirty One

Dressed in all black like the omen, today I decided to face all the pain. I was tired of running and hiding, my transformation was starting today!

I drove Lynda's rental car to Rico's funeral, since I no longer had one. I pulled up out front and it was like a reunion or party, everybody was there. I got out the car and prepared myself for the worst. I knew everyone was waiting on me, just to have something to talk about. I walked up to the casket and was happy it was closed casket. I didn't think my heart could stand seeing him laying there before me.

"You were my first, my heart and will always remain my everything. I love you Rico Smith." I kissed his casket, and turned away. I walked up to his mom and sister and gave them each a hug. There was a caramel colored baby boy sitting on his mother's lap. "Aww, he is adorable. Whose baby is this?"

"This is Rico Jr.," his sister said kissing him on his cheek.

"Rico's what?" I said surprised.

"His son," Kristin said walking up behind me.

"His son's mother is in the restroom. He's two months and looks just like his dad," Rico's mother said kissing the baby on his forehead.

I nodded my head in agreement with her but I really didn't want to hear that news.

"What are you doing here?" Kristin insisted on nagging me.

"I loved him just as much as you say you did. Far as this baby business that was something he kept from me, not to hurt me," I whispered in her ear, trying my best not to cause a scene.

"He lied to you because he didn't care, stupid," she said walking away.

I sat in the back through the service and didn't look to my left or right. I kept my eyes glued on the casket. I wanted to talk to him one last time. I couldn't believe that he had a baby and I didn't know anything about it. Maybe Kristin was right. I dipped out of the service before it ended.

As I was walking back to the car I saw Cliff standing with a few more cops. They were leaning against a police car.

"On duty at a funeral, huh?"

"Yeah, I have to make sure everything and everybody is okay."

"Everybody or just me?" I laughed. I knew that Cliff could help me with the last step in my plan. The worse he could say was no, so I gave it a shot.

"Cliff, I need a favor. I know you have gone above and beyond the call of duty for me but I really need your help on this." I was praying he went for it. I knew this would bring an end to my beef with Joe.

"What's up?" he was all ears.

"I need to see Joe. I know that's asking a lot but I really need to see him." I went over my plan with him and he listened intently.

"Man, you better not go in there on no bullshit. Meet me downtown in an hour," he warned me. He gave me a look that said he meant business and I agreed.

On my way to my car, I saw Rico's baby mother walking out holding the baby. She was pretty and I looked her up and down. "What does she have that he didn't see in me?" I pulled my glasses down a little bit to get a better view of her. I was so hurt because he had been dealing with someone all along. Someone other than Kirstin.

Going all the way home would have been a waste of time, so I just made my way downtown. I was stressing so bad that I started to feel sick. I pulled over on the side of the freeway because I felt nauseated. I felt like I was going to throw up as I leaned out of the window letting the air hit my face. I finally got myself together and pulled up in front of the county jail.

I waited thirty minutes before Cliff walked up to my car. "Come on," he said tapping on the hood.

"Where did you come from?" I said running behind him trying to catch up.

"Just come on. Now you know you aren't old enough to see him; so act like he is your brother and he is your guardian." He was running down the plan to me and I was listening to every word.

"Okay, I got you." I walked into the building and they search me like I was coming to blow the place up.

"ID," the man said after he checked my purse.

"She's with me," Cliff said to the guard. "Her brother is here and he is her only guardian. He has the keys to their house and she can't get in," he kept explaining himself and I stood on the side of him.

"She's clear," the guard told the lady behind the desk so she could buzz me into the back.

"Let's go," Cliff said. I walked close behind him. I was actually scared. The county was dirty and nasty. I tried my best not to touch anything, not even the buttons on the elevator.

"Joseph Sanders," Cliff said to another guard that had to go get him from his cell.

"Wow, they have guards everywhere in here."

"Yeah, trust me they're needed," he said turning to me as the gate opened.

"Go ahead," he pointed to the entry and I turned and looked at him if he was crazy.

"You're not going with me?" I said thinking Joe was crazy even if he was in jail, that man was no one to play with.

"No, this is your business to handle, not mine."

I walked into a room that was divided by a glass wall with small cubicles for visiting. There was a phone of both sides. Joe immediately went wild when he saw me.

"What the fuck you want?" Joe snapped.

"Call your squad off of me and my moms." I wanted to let him know I wasn't about to let him over talk me.

"What squad? Ain't nobody thinking about you or your moms, man," he said laughing. "Seems to me I'm not the only one you fucked over." He placed his hand on his chin and leaned closer to the glass that separated us.

"First off, I didn't fuck over anyone. You used me as your personal punching bag; and in return I used you for your money. The day you left, I didn't know that was a set up so stop telling people I did."

"Bitch you did! You knew that nigga," he got loud and I knew if the glass wasn't there he would have really put his hands on me.

"You're right, I did. That was my first and only love; and what did you do? You took him away from me, and you lied to people, thinking I was a part of it all." My emotions were starting to take over, and I was holding back tears.

"You were with me day and day out. You are who you hang around; so you are just as guilty as I am," he smirked when he said that.

"No I'm not, and if that's so then you're the snitch. You were running around town with a cop, working with the enemy huh?" I knew I had the upper hand, and I was about to run with it. "Now you want to play dirty, because we can. Now leave me and my mother alone or I will make your reputation a living hell."

As I turned around to walk off, I could hear him still talking. "I keep telling you I'm not the only one who has it out for you," he screamed.

I continued to walk down the hall. I knew a man's name was everything to him. He couldn't live with himself knowing that the streets wouldn't respect him. My work was done and I knew I didn't have to worry about Joe any longer.

"Thank you," I shook Cliff's hand and was happy that chapter of my life was over. I was giving it up completely. I walked outside and was feeling myself. This was my new beginning. I was happy but I still felt like hell. I leaned over by Lynda's car and started vomiting again.

After picking Lynda up from work, I returned home to my bed and slept the day away. When I woke up I grabbed my grandmother's journal and thought it was time to add to the tradition.

I called my passage, "Facing the Pain."

Tears from many unshed moments, unshared times unloved feelings hurt fills my heart followed by pain. I maintain no man they all came and went leaving me to face more rainy days and finding unhealthy ways to cover it. My true colors were hidden, I wouldn't know them if I came face to face with them. I lost myself long ago when I built a new me to survive in these streets, which now had become my home but I have walked away looking for shelter, looking for help to rebuild my new character. I turn to God and tell myself no man stands a chance next to him and that's who I'm running too!

Chapter Thirty Two

"I'm sorry. I did it to hurt you. Kristin was just to get back at you," Rico wiped my tears as he saw them fall.

"I know you didn't mean to hurt me, but you did. I hate that I love you so much."

I walked to him and hugged him. Forgiveness was the key to any love and I was willing to let it go. I felt a sharp pain in my stomach and was at it again… "Ma…" I called out waking up from my dream vomiting on the side of my bed.

"Oh, my goodness! Let me get a towel." She came running just like she did when I was a kid. I couldn't even get the strength to sit all the way up. My stomach felt like it was in knots.

"Can you please get me some water?" I said holding my mouth with my hands.

"Girl, I don't know what you got, but I hope I don't catch it. I just got this new job and I can't be getting sick. Today is your birthday and you in here sick." She touched my forehead making sure I didn't have a fever. It was June and I was hoping I didn't have the flu.

"The phone has been ringing off the hook for you." She passed it to me, and I read the caller ID. Kiyah, Dig and Jade had all called.

"Well, I'm off to work. Call me if you need me. Miss. Alice is next door, call her if it's emergency," Lynda said walking out my room.

"Alright," I rolled onto my back on my bed, and touched my stomach. I can't believe I'm feeling like this." I looked down at my stomach and that's when it hit me. "Rico didn't use a condom. Oh my god!"

I jumped up and went to the bathroom and ran the shower. I needed to get to the doctor ASAP.

"Birthday Girl…it's Kiy and Jade. What you doing today?" I was finally eighteen but it really wasn't a big deal to me. I had been grown for a long time now.

"Nothing ladies. I'm really not feeling too good. I think I'm going to stay in." I wanted to tell Kiyah so bad, but I knew she wouldn't understand.

"Well we will stop by and bring our gifts over later," Kiyah said. Thank God because I was going to have to find a way to get rid of them.

"No…I mean that's okay you don't have to get me anything." I said wrapping my towel around me.

"Girl bye, we will be over by five," she said hanging up.

"Fuck," I screamed out, sitting on my bed putting on my bra and panties. I stood up and looked into my full sized mirror. I looked fine, I didn't look pregnant. I flopped back down on the bed and couldn't even think of anyone to call to take me to the doctor. I was always running to Kiyah for things, but this time it was different. I couldn't have her knowing I had slept with that boy unprotected knowing he was sleeping with any and everybody.

This was yet another situation catching up with me. I had slept with Rico that night to get back at him and Kristin and once again I had only brought pain to myself. Now I might be carrying his seed.

"Dig, are you busy?" I asked hoping he wasn't.

"Naw at home chilling, you okay?" he was always concerned about me.

"Not really. I don't feel good at all and my Mom is gone to work. I need a way to the hospital." I started feeling queasy again and was running back to the bathroom.

"Ohh…" I said holding my face over the toilet.

"Monnie, I will be over in a minute."

I hung the phone up and sat it on the floor as I continued to hurl over the toilet. Minutes later Dig was knocking at the front door. It took me almost five minutes to get to the door.

"Hey," I opened the door and walked away making my way to the kitchen to get something to put on my stomach.

"Happy Birthday," Dig said handing me a card.

"Wow…you really didn't have to get my anything." I said still accepting the card. I read the card carefully and it explained the true meaning of friendship.

"Thank you." I was putting the card back inside and I noticed a $100 bill. "Thank you so much, Dig." I reached up and hugged him.

"You welcome man. You think you grown now don't you?" He joked.

"No not really. I wish I could go back to being a kid," I said eating a piece of toast and drinking some water. "But I'm ready," I grabbed my purse and we headed out.

We walked into Henry Ford and I was nervous as hell. The worst part was that there wasn't a doubt in my mind that I wasn't pregnant. I knew I was, and I knew this was pay back.

"Ar'monnie Wright," they called me to the back soon as I signed in. This was a first because usually you would have to be in there for about two hours before you saw a doctor.

"You going to sit out here?" I turned back and asked Dig as I was walking off.

"I didn't think you wanted me to come back." He got up and walked behind me into the blue door.

Reality

"You can wait in there. The doctor will be right with you," the nurse said after she weighed me and checked my blood pressure.

"You feel like you have to throw up?" Dig asked sitting in the chair that was in my room.

"Not now," I said rubbing my stomach. I was here to get confirmation for what I already knew.

"Hello, I'm Dr. Cloche," the doctor said walking knocking on the door and coming in before we said anything.

"Hi," I said thinking finally I was ready to know what exactly was going on with me.

"Now what brings you in today?" she was looking over my chart, waiting on me to answer.

I was tired of playing with my own head and others; so I told the truth. "I think I may be pregnant." I was ready to call it like I see it, and I was going to own up to the plate.

"Really?" the doctor and Dig said at the same time. He looked as if he had just choked on his own spit.

"Yes," I said inhaling and exhaling.

"Well let's get some blood work and we will get this all taken care of."

I followed her out to the nurse station and let her stick me over and over until she could get some of my blood. I walked back in the room with Dig while we waited. If I wasn't pregnant this sure was a helluva stomach virus.

"So it's Joe's baby?" Dig asked like that was just eating him up inside.

"No we never even slept together. I told ya'll it was all business with him." I wondered if he believed me. Most people thought if a girl was talking to someone they just had to be sleeping together.

"Yeah alright." That little smart remark he said made me know right then, he didn't.

"Well congrats you two!" Dr. Cloche yelled entering the room.

"What?" I covered my mouth and felt like I had to throw up all over again.

"That ain't my baby," Dig assured her.

"Oh, will you be needing a blood test soon?" she asked looking at me as if I should have been embarrassed.

"No, what he means is that we are not an item, we're just friends!" I cut my eyes at him so he could know I was mad.

"Well you have a lot of options, so I'll be sure to have the nurse give you a pamphlet before you leave," she said handing me my papers.

I began to cry as soon as she left the room. Dig sprang into action, "Man I got you. I swear I do and I don't care who the daddy is. You are going to be taken care of," Dig grabbed my head and placed it on his chest.

"No, this is why I'm in the predicament I'm in now. I was so used to having someone take care of me; that I never knew how to stand on my own two feet. I had to learn the hard way, and I made all bad choices and it's all catching up to me now. This is real. I'm not a little girl anymore."

I wrapped my arms around his shoulders and squeezed him, it felt good again to be in a guy arms. A guy that really cared about me and loved me. Not just for my looks or body but for me.

"I love you, Dig," I backed up and looked up at him.

"I love you too. Let's get out of here."

We walked out and as I passed the nurse she handed me my pamphlets. On my way home I looked through it and abortion to me was my only way out.

"Get some rest call me if you need me," Dig said pulling up at my house.

"I will…" I exited the car and as usual Miss. Alice was sitting on the porch. I couldn't even hold my head up to speak to her. I felt I had let her down as well as myself, yet again.

For the next two days I didn't accept any calls from anyone. I stayed in my bed and cried. I didn't eat, barely got any sleep and just wanted all the pain and hurt to end.

Lynda was back at it like before, working like crazy so she would check on me and be right back out the door.

Lying in that bed gave me time to think and time to pray. I asked God to please steer me in the right direction and three days later I was where I felt I should be.

Chapter Thirty Three

I couldn't help but wonder how I'd gotten myself into this situation. As I sat in the sterile, all white room tremors of fear ran through my body. I couldn't be mad at anyone but myself. I had been through so much in my eighteen years; if I told the story to anyone would think I was at least twenty-five.

My leg started to shake as I watched the door knob turn. My time had come….

As I walked into the room I felt I was walking into the devil's plan. I had let myself get to the lowest point of my life, and I didn't want to bring a child into my web of mistakes. I needed to take control of my life and get back on track.

"Here you are, you can change in there," the nurse said handing me a change of clothes to put on.

"Um...I think I need more time. I'm not sure this is what I want to do." I handed her back the clothes making my way out the door.

When I walked back into the lobby, it was filled with young girls who had made mistakes just like I had. I only hoped that this experience would make them see what I had. It was time for change.

I walked out onto Seven mile going to the parking lot when I noticed there was a white note attached to my window. I opened the note and it read, "*Remember one who does wrong, must not go unpunished.*"

I brushed it off, and jumped into my truck.

On my way home I listened to T.I "Still ain't forgave myself," and thought of what my cousin Kyle always said, 'What goes around comes around.' I knew my days were going to catch up to me, but I was not prepared for the storm that was ahead.

I parked my mother's car in the back once I was home. I had built my courage up and was going to tell my mother everything I had done, and was planning to do to get myself together. I was going to lay it on the line from start to finish.

I felt I owed it to Rico. I still felt responsible for his death; and I didn't want to be the reason his seed didn't make it to breathe either. Even though he had hurt me in every way possible, I still loved him and wished he was still here. I wondered if he was here, would he have wanted me to keep the baby.

My thoughts were broken when I heard a knock at the door. I thought it couldn't have been anybody but Miss. Alice. Lynda had her checking in on me like I was five. I opened the door and no one was there. I looked around and there was another note that said the exact same thing as the others. It was starting to creep me out. The only person I could think that would be up to this was Joe.

"He's just not going to leave me alone," I said slamming the door closed. Then there was a knock at the back door. I raced to it knowing whoever it was couldn't get away that fast, when I opened it I started going off.

"I know Joe sent you and you a coward because you won't show who you are," I continued walking onto the porch more. I looked down and saw a shadow behind me. I turned around quickly.

"What the fuck?" was all I could get out before I was getting hit upside the head with a Desert Eagle.

"Shut up! You will pay," the man said firing my body up with shots. He shot me five times before he turned away. Through blurry eyes I saw him get into a black truck that pulled up in the alley behind the house. I saw my unborn child, Rico and my cousin's flash before me. I laid there unable to move. The pain was terrible. I hoped someone would save me. I started calling his name. The one person I should have called on since day one…GOD.

I hated that I was going to die with people thinking bad of me. I wanted my chance to change. I wanted people to know the new me. I knew I wasn't living, I had just been existing. My life wasn't holding any purpose, which was why I didn't cherish it. I begged God to come take this pain away. I wanted to live!

"Forgive me Father for I have sinned. Take me back let me be born again!" was the only prayer I was strong enough to get out before I was gone.

My days were clipped and my life was cut. I didn't think I would ever see day light again. Her voice struck me waking me up, which I followed back home.

"Monnie."

I opened my eyes and my angel stood there. Lynda was on the side of the bed holding my hand, crying happily to see my eyes open.

"Baby, I love you," she said kissing on my face. The word baby reminded me of my own. I touched my stomach and tried to sit up but couldn't.

"No sweetie, the baby is gone. It didn't survive." Her tears fell as she laid her head on my stomach. I cried wishing I would have died. I would have rather my life been taken so my child could have lived.

"Ma..." I spoke softly and low, grabbing her hand tight. I needed her more than ever. I felt completely drained. No pain could have compared to this. I lost my child; due to the life I was living. Someone wanted revenge on me just as much as I wanted it on anyone who I had felt did me wrong. Karma was truly a bitch, and I didn't blame anyone but myself.

I let my head hit the pillow and closed my eyes. I pictured my child. The same vision I had when I was lying on the ground lifeless, the same vision I had when I called on God. "I'm so sorry. I know you are still living." The tears fell and at the moment I knew my child, my flesh and blood was still living, just above me in heaven.

"Yes he or she is and will always be living through you," Lynda said kissing me on my forehead. We held on to each other and knew that all we had was each other. I didn't let her arm go that entire night. I didn't want anyone but her. I now understood the love for a child. To love is to want happiness for each other, safety and peace. My child had that now!

I was in the hospital for two weeks. The day I came home, I went to register for school. I was happy to get into a fast track program that would help me to graduate on time. I still had a chance. I wasn't only doing this for myself, it was for my baby and Rico. See people pick and choose what they believe is good for them, but they sometimes never stop to think how their actions will affect anyone else.

I became selfish and my lifestyle took over my actions and better judgment. My bitter ways took me on a journey that I would always remember but never let define who I am or where I'm going.

When I returned home, Lynda and I felt like the whole neighborhoods eyes were on us.

"Guess everybody knows what happened huh?" I said walking on the porch.

"Yeah, but oh well. Everyone is going to have their opinions," she said unlocking the door.

"I don't care Ma," and I honestly didn't care. I used to care so much about what people thought of me because I wasn't comfortable with myself. Now I'm at a point in my life where I know I have grown, and I'm at peace. Words no longer mattered to me.

Chapter Thirty Four

"This is going to be a long ride," I yawned letting my seat back. I was trying to get my thoughts together I was on my way to see Ricardo. I didn't know what to expect, but he begged my mother to bring me. My getting shot woke a lot of people up.

"Not really," Lynda said pushing it already and we wasn't even on the freeway yet. I was happy again. I learned things being in the hospital, the three people who loved me outside of family was Kiyah, Dig and Jade. They were the friends holding their breath until they knew I was fine.

Cliff was on the case and told Lynda he wasn't going to rest until he found out who had shot me. I asked him what to do with all the money he helped me take from Joe's house that night, and he answered me using one of his favorite quotes. "It's your life, live it how you want too." I took that as he was telling me take it and spend it how I want to.

The old Ar'monnie would have blown it, but I was thinking about the long haul. I was going to put it aside for school and a car of my own. I told myself I was ready to live, and have meaning to each and every day of my life. I stared out the window thinking of all my plans, nothing like the old ones. I was thinking straight.

"Monnie we're here." She must have thought I was asleep.

"Why you so loud? I'm up," I said getting out of the car. I looked around and the prison looked just like they did in the movies,

After about thirty minutes of being searched and waiting on them to go get him, I was walking into my cousins arms.

"Oh my God." I was surprised that I didn't let myself cry. I hugged him and it was like my heart was smiling. I felt like that sixteen year old girl again.

"I missed you, man," he said hugging me just as tight as I was hugging him.

"You know we have to kick it," he said walking towards my mother but still looking at me.

"I know…I know…" after about an hour of family talk, Lynda was at the vending machine and Ricardo and I were left alone.

"So what's up little girl?" he smiled and said hitting me on the leg.

"Nothing, I'm going back to school…" I knew he would happy to hear that, probably not knowing I ever stopped.

"Yeah I heard, but tell me this and I'm not trying to judge you or make you feel bad. I just want to know what was your motive for everything, because I need to know. Keep in mind I know everything from the day we left up to now." His smile dropped and I knew he wanted the honest truth.

"To cover up the pain. To keep acting as if nothing fazed me. I wanted everyone around me to hurt like I did when ya'll left, but everything just did a 360 on me. I never meant for it to blow out of proportion. I just was trying to live and make things happen."

We saw Lynda making her way back, but she didn't sit too close. I believe she knew he was having that cousin to cousin talk with me.

"See the thing about the game is, you never know in them streets if today is your last day or not. You have to be smart and sometimes they can out smart you, look at me. Just go back to school. I'm proud of you for that. Remember it's not about who makes it the fastest, it's about who last the longest. You see people can get on top quick as hell, but fall right back down because they didn't know how to be humble and hold onto their spot. Go to school get to the top, and keep going."

"I got you, Cuzo," was all I could say after that. The rest of the visit went okay. I slept the whole ride home, and needed the rest. I started school Monday and Dig and I were going out to lunch. He was a bit down, after finding out Ryan's baby wasn't his. I was going to be there for him just like he had always been for me.

I pulled out my grandmother's journal and began to write:

Losing yourself is far worse than losing any material thing, or person. You get so far into the fast money and the fast life that you lose sight of everything that is before you. You surround yourself with anyone who shows you attention, anyone who spends money on you. You have sex just to hear someone say they love you or to feel special. Not knowing that treatment must come from within. Drinking and smoking just so the problems could fade away, but once the smoke clears the problems re appear. My Reality was always near but I was too blind and couldn't see clear. I was running from pain only to gain more, now I'm standing alone knocking at God's door. He has given me a second chance and it is truly going to be one I endure!

I placed the journal back in my memory box and climbed into bed. I closed my eyes and this night I prayed not to have a dream about the shooting. It would always replay in my head, and I would never miss a beat but it was one detail I caught tonight that I hadn't before! The black truck he jumped into after he shot me, there was a woman driving. I only knew one lady in town with that truck. I saw the vision again and this time I saw her face. "KRISTIN!" I yelled jumping up out of my sleep. I had underestimated her.

BETRAYAL

"Chino, I thought I told you to kill her. I'm not paying you the rest of your money until you finish the job," Kristin said hanging up. Kristin hadn't felt a bit of sympathy when she'd heard Ar'monnie had lost her child. She wanted her dead and wasn't going to stop until it was done.

"This bitch will get what's coming to her!" Kristin burned the last picture she had of her old friend which was now her enemy number one.

ORDER FORM

To place mail orders, please send money orders payable to Shanaetris Edwards to:

Shanaetris Edwards

P.O. Box 6493

Detroit, MI 48206

14.99 + tax (MI sales tax 6%) = 15.89

Turnaround time is 5-7 business days.

Number of Books _____ x $14.99 ______________

Tax ______________

Subtotal: ______________

Shipping & Handling $2.85 ______________

Total: ______________

Shipping Information (REQUIRED)

Name:____

Address:____

City:_______________ State:_________ Zip:__________

Contact Number (optional):_______________________

Email :____

Your support is appreciated!

ORDER FORM

To place mail orders, please send money orders payable to Shanaetris Edwards to:

Shanaetris Edwards

P.O. Box 6493

Detroit, MI 48206

14.99 + tax (MI sales tax 6%) = 15.89

Turnaround time is 5-7 business days.

Number of Books _____ x $14.99 ____________

Tax ____________

Subtotal: ____________

Shipping & Handling $2.85 ____________

Total: ____________

Shipping Information (REQUIRED)

Name:____

Address:______________________________________

City:______________ State:_________ Zip:_________

Contact Number (optional):______________________

Email :____

Your support is appreciated!

Breinigsville, PA USA
16 February 2011
255585BV00005B/2/P